Daughter of War

Daughter of War

A NOVEL

Marsha Forchuk Skrypuch

Fitzhenry & Whiteside

Copyright © 2008 by Marsha Forchuk Skrypuch

Published in Canada by Fitzhenry & Whiteside,
195 Allstate Parkway, Markham, Ontario L3R 4T8

Published in the United States by Fitzhenry & Whiteside,
311 Washington Street, Brighton, Massachusetts 02135

www.fitzhenry.ca   godwit@fitzhenry.ca

10 9 8 7 6 5 4 3 2 1

Library and Archives Canada Cataloguing in Publication

Skrypuch, Marsha Forchuk, 1954-
Daughter of war / Marsha Forchuk Skrypuch.
ISBN 978-1-55455-044-9

1. Armenian massacres, 1915-1923—Juvenile fiction. I. Title.
PS8587.K79D39 2008   jC813'.54   C2007-907008-6

U.S. Publisher Cataloging-in-Publication Data
(Library of Congress Standards)

Skrypuch, Marsha Forchuk, 1954-
Daughter of war / Marsha Forchuk Skrypuch.
[214] p. : cm.
Summary: After surviving the Armenian genocide in Turkey during World War I, a
teenager disguised as an Arab undertakes a dangerous journey back to Turkey to
reunite with his betrothed and her sister, who was sold into slavery.
ISBN: 978-155-455044-9 (pbk.)
1. Armenian massacres, 1915-1923 — Juvenile fiction. I. Title.
[Fic] dc22   PZ7.S62853Dau 2008

Fitzhenry & Whiteside acknowledges with thanks the Canada Council for the Arts and the
Ontario Arts Council for their support of our publishing program. We acknowledge the financial
support of the Government of Canada through the Book Publishing Industry Development
Program (BPIDP) for our publishing activities.

 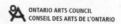

Canada Council   Conseil des Arts
for the Arts   du Canada

ONTARIO ARTS COUNCIL
CONSEIL DES ARTS DE L'ONTARIO

Designed by Fortunato Design Inc.

Cover image by Chris Bradley / Axiom Photographic Agency / Getty Images

Printed in Canada

For my sister, Cheryl

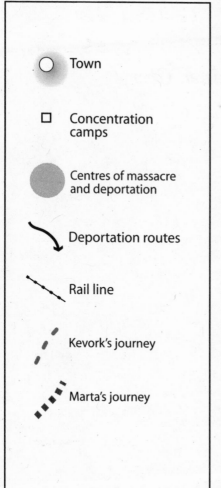

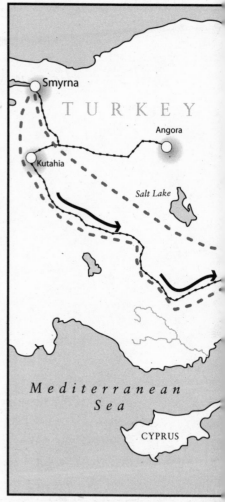

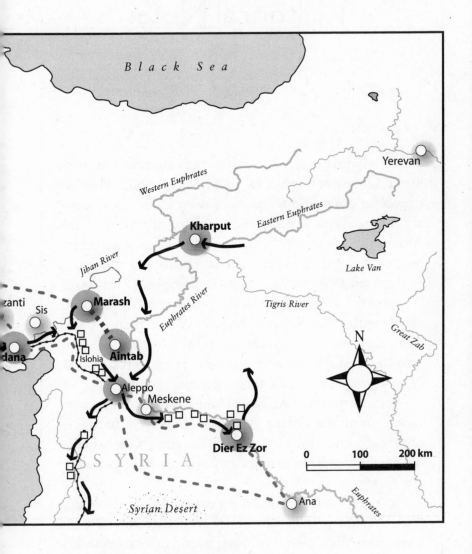

Historical Note

The early part of the 20th century was a tumultuous time in the Ottoman Empire. In 1908, Sultan Abdul Hamid's crumbling government was overthrown by the revolutionary Young Turks. Minorities, including the largest—the Armenians—were initially in favor of this new government because it promised to bring about equality and reforms.

In April 1909, the Sultan briefly came back into power. A massacre of Armenians in the province of Adana coincided with the Sultan's return. More than 30,000 Armenians were slaughtered within a matter of days. Thousands of Armenian homes were burnt to the ground. No one was punished for these atrocities.

Some orphaned Armenian children did manage to escape from the Adana Massacre. Some ended up in orphanages run by German missionaries. One notable orphanage complex was in the city of Marash, in southeastern Turkey.

In 1913, a new political wing emerged from the Young Turk movement. This new entity was called the CUP, the Committee for Union and Progress, and it seized power in 1913. The CUP developed a policy of "Turkey for the Turks."

They wanted to get rid of the minorities and expand into the Russian territory where Turkish people lived. During World War I, the CUP formed an alliance with Germany and Austria-Hungary.

During World War I, Armenians were forced to join the Turkish Army. Some, alarmed by the CUP's policies, crossed the border to Russia and fought against Turkey.

Beginning in the spring of 1915, the Turkish government drove the Armenians from their homes. Under the guise of "relocation," entire Armenian communities were marched hundreds of miles into the Syrian Desert without food or water. Death by thirst, malnutrition, and exhaustion was common. Others were shot. In all, more than one million Armenians died.

Armenian children who lived in the German orphanages were supposed to be safe from deportation, but any who were considered adult suffered the same fate as other Armenians.

Compassionate Muslim families rescued many children from the lines of marching Armenians and brought them up as Muslims. Some of the younger women survived the death march when they were taken into Muslim homes as concubines and slaves. Other Armenians were rescued by nomadic Arabs who lived in the desert. Disguised, these few survivors lived in constant fear that one day they would be discovered and shot or marched into the desert to die.

Daughter of War tells the story of two Armenian sisters, Mariam and Marta, who are rescued by Turks. It is also the story of Kevork, a young Armenian man who is rescued by an Arab clan. But after rescue, what then? How do you rebuild a life after everything—even your identity—has been taken from you? And how do you find out if any of your loved ones have survived as well?

This story is based on firsthand accounts of the Armenian Genocide in Turkey during the First World War. The characters are fictionalized with the exception of Leslie A. Davis, who was an American consul. His observations were published in 1989 in *The Slaughterhouse Province: An American Diplomat's Report on the Armenian Genocide, 1915-1917.*

One

KEVORK

Kevork rubbed the last remnants of sleep from his eyes with the back of his free hand as he balanced his rucksack in the other. He walked through the covered bazaar to his own tiny stall. The sun had barely begun to peek out over the horizon, and the first call to prayer of the day had just finished. But Kevork wasn't the first one there. Inhaling the heady aroma of cloves and cinnamon, he passed Diya al Din's spice stand. He watched his step to make sure he didn't trip over one of Ghalib's chickens. Kevork was so anxious for an early start that he hadn't even taken time to break his fast, so when he passed Radhiya's baking pit, the smell of freshly baked flat bread made his stomach growl.

Radhiya's veiled head emerged from the cloth flap of the baking pit. Droplets of sweat glistened on her upper lip. She grinned. "Here's one for you," she said, holding a smoking hot flat bread between two calloused fingers.

Kevork drew out a coin from his pocket and placed it on the counter.

"Thank you," he answered in Arabic as he grabbed the hot bread and held it gingerly in his hand.

From the day he had arrived in January, the other stall owners had accepted Kevork at face value. If they'd known who he really was, they'd never let on. But then again, why would they? Yes, he

1

was still in his teens, but his skin had darkened and become wrinkled during his time in the desert. His adoptive clan had tattooed his face with the group's distinctive small blue dot on each temple, and he had a single crosshatched line of blue around his right wrist. He had also begun to carry a small unadorned prayer mat. Five times a day he would stop what he was doing, position his prayer mat to face Mecca, and pray. Aleppo was a mostly Arab city, and Kevork fit right in.

He set the leather satchel onto the dusty ground and untied the flaps covering his booth to indicate that he was open for business. He placed the satchel on his workbench and drew out the implements of his shoemaker's trade: a small hammer, sturdy needles, waxed leather thread, a shoe form, and pieces of leather.

Mostly Kevork mended sandals. Aleppo bordered the desert, after all.

Whenever he got the chance to make a pair of sandals from scratch, Kevork's heart soared at the novelty. So when the American had showed up a week ago asking for a new pair of boots, Kevork hadn't believed his luck. Even more miraculous was the fact that the American wanted to travel north, stopping in Marash, Turkey, before moving on to the remote Turkish town of Harput. Kevork had excitedly volunteered to be his guide, and the American had agreed. He had paid for the boots in advance and suggested that Kevork might want to make a pair for himself as well because their trip would be arduous. Kevork hadn't worn boots since the deportation.

Kevork unwrapped the beautiful new boots that he had made for the American. When would he pick them up? He held them to his face and breathed in the scent of fresh leather.

Kevork's mind flitted back a year ago to another special pair of boots that he had made—for her.

They walked side by side to the shoemaker's workshop at the Marash orphanage. When they got inside, Kevork closed and locked the door.

"Sit," he said, pointing to one of the work stools.

Marta sat.

Kevork leaned forward and clasped her hands. "I wanted to marry you."

Marta blinked back tears and nodded.

He let go of her hands, walked over to a bundle on the shelf, and presented it to her.

"This was to be my betrothal gift to you."

Marta looked in wonder from the bundle to Kevork's eyes. "Then I shouldn't open it."

"Times are different," he said. "You'll need these." And with that, he flipped open the cloth.

Marta's eyes widened when she saw the handmade boots. "They're beautiful," she breathed.

"I only wish I could have given them to you under happier circumstances."

She reached out her hand and touched one of the boots with her fingertip as if to make sure it was real. She stuck out her feet. The boots she wore were a tattered mess.

He knelt down in front of her and drew her old boots off. Then he reverently slipped on the newly made boots.

"Stand up," he said.

Marta stood up. She peered down at her new boots with a sad smile. She wrapped her arms around Kevork's neck. "Thank you," she said and kissed him on his bottom lip.

Kevork held her close. "I will protect you."

"They could separate us," Marta said.

Kevork swallowed back his tears.

"I won't let them," he said fiercely.

"You may not have a choice," she said.

He took a deep breath and let the air out slowly. "If we are parted," he said, "I pledge that I will find a way to get back here."

Marta looked up into his face. He was shocked by the coldness in her eyes. "If we're separated…" She stood on her toes and kissed him on both lips. "I will come back here or die trying."

The memory filled Kevork's eyes with tears. Marta had been fourteen, and he was a year older.

They had now been separated for a year. Was she dead or alive?

"Can this be fixed?"

Kevork was startled out of his musings. He glanced up. An unveiled woman with a look of distrust in her kohl-darkened eyes held out one beaded sandal. Kevork took it from her and turned it this way and that, examining it closely. It was an Aleppo *kab-kab*, a leather and wooden clog favored by locals. The kab-kab had been carefully decorated with seed beads in red, blue, and yellow, and sewn in an intricate swirling pattern. He turned the clog upside down. The wood had split so badly that the clog was nearly in two pieces.

"It could be glued," said Kevork as he ran his finger along the fault. "But it is sure to split again, the more you walk on it."

"So it can't be fixed?" she asked.

"Is it the beadwork you wish to save?" asked Kevork.

The woman nodded.

"Then I could make a new wooden base and sew the old upper back on." Kevork set the kab-kab back down on the counter. "Do you have its mate?"

"Yes," said the woman.

Then she drew a second kab-kab from the folds of her dress and handed it to Kevork. He turned it upside down and held it up close to his face, squinting. "This one is about to split too," he said. He prodded the nail of his index finger into a hairline crack and held it up to the woman.

"Then we'd better fix both," said the woman. "How much will that be?"

"Much cheaper than a new pair." Kevork grinned. "I will have them ready for you in two days."

From the corner of his eye, he saw a Turkish soldier a few booths down. Kevork willed his hand to remain steady as he finished the woman's receipt and handed it to her. Soldiers were an increasing presence in Aleppo of late. Why was this one in the market?

Kevork smiled and nodded at the woman as she turned to go. Then he quickly busied himself by picking up one of his needles and threading it. He forced himself to look unconcerned as the soldier approached. He prayed that the soldier would walk on. But just as he was tugging the tip of the narrow waxed leather through the eye of the needle, the soldier stopped in front of his booth and slammed down a polished wooden rifle with a clatter.

Kevork's heart was pounding so hard that he thought it would burst out of his chest. Had this soldier somehow seen through his Arab disguise? Kevork set the needle and thread down, hoping that the soldier wouldn't notice his trembling hands.

"May I help you?" asked Kevork.

"The strap is gone," said the soldier. "Can you make me a new one?"

Kevork looked into the soldier's eyes and smiled. "I'm sure I can help you," he said.

He gazed down at the rifle, trying not to speculate where it had been used. Kevork's fingertips brushed along the polished wooden barrel until it reached the midway point, where one end of the leather strap was usually attached to a metal ring. The ring was bent but still serviceable. He ran his fingertips down to the butt of the rifle and examined the other strap holder. It was in perfect condition.

"It's just the strap itself I need," said the soldier. "Can you fix it now?"

"I can cut you a new strap in a matter of minutes," said Kevork. "But I have no black leather—only brown."

"But you can make a new strap and attach it?" asked the soldier.

"Yes."

"Then get to it," said the soldier, leaning on the counter with both elbows. "I'll wait while you do it."

That was the last thing Kevork wanted. His heart was already pounding so hard that he thought he might faint. How long could he keep up this calm facade?

Kevork pulled out a length of sturdy brown bull hide. He measured, marked the desired length on the back of the hide with a bit of chalk, and cut out the strap with a razor-sharp knife. Then he inserted the rivets at either end of the strap.

"I'll need the rifle to attach the strap," said Kevork, gingerly reaching for the weapon.

"Here," said the soldier, handing it over. "It's not loaded." He looked mildly interested as he watched Kevork hammer the rivets shut.

Kevork tugged at the strap to make sure it was firmly in place. He handed the rifle back to the soldier, who grinned with delight.

"They told me you were good," he said. "And they were right." The soldier reached into his pocket and drew out some coins. He dropped them on the counter and left.

Kevork was dizzy with relief as he watched the soldier exit the bazaar. Then he looked down at the soldier's payment. Amidst the coins was a simple brass wedding ring. It was the kind that his mother had worn. Had the soldier taken it from an Armenian corpse?

Kevork's hands trembled again as he packed up his stall for the night. Of all the shoemakers in Aleppo, why had *he* been chosen? Maybe it was just a coincidence. But if the soldier knew, Kevork was no longer safe.

But was anywhere safe when you were Armenian?

Two

MARTA

"You're coming with me."

Marta looked up, startled. Idris, the first wife, had climbed up to the rooftop and now stood in front of her, hands on hips, a furrow of determination on her brow.

"Where are we going?" asked Marta. She had been scrubbing a particularly stubborn stain out of the husband's favorite vest. She dunked it in the rinse water one more time and wrung it out.

"Some place where you can no longer cause mischief," replied Idris. "Finish that up," she added, pointing to the vest, "then come." Idris turned and walked down the wooden steps into the house.

Marta carefully laid the vest on the hot metal rooftop to dry. She stood up and wiped her hands on the front of her coarse cotton tunic. She felt the bulge in her abdomen. Was this the mischief Idris had referred to?

Marta followed Idris down the steps.

The husband was gone, of course. He had left hours ago for the market.

Adila, the second wife and ten years younger than the first, sat cross-legged on the floor, her fingers moving deftly as they wove yet another of her prized reed baskets. She looked up briefly from her work to tip her head in acknowledgment to First Wife. Then she silently regarded Marta for a moment with a fleeting look of sadness.

"Get into your chador," said Idris. "Then carry those sacks to the wagon."

The first sack Marta lifted was fairly light. She breathed in a mixture of spices—saffron, curry, cinnamon. Her hands could feel the outline of bread, dried fruit, and other staples. As she carried it outside, a rented wooden oxcart arrived. The driver leaned against the side of the cart and popped a handful of roasted chickpeas into his mouth. He nodded a greeting.

The cart was packed with wooden crates and sacks. Marta found a space for the sack and then went back into the house for the other one. The second sack was much heavier. As she placed her arms around it, she could feel the thick outline of the bolts of cloth. Pain shot through Marta's back as she lifted the sack and struggled outside with it. The driver scrambled to help her as she pushed the bundle into the back of the wagon, but Idris waved him away.

"My slave girl needs the exercise."

The ox driver helped Idris up to the bench. He walked around to the driver's side and hoisted himself up. Marta stood there, wondering what to do.

"In there. Quickly," said Idris, flicking her finger at the back of the cart. Marta looked with dismay at the tightly packed cart. She had barely scrambled up when the cart began to move. She grabbed on to one of the larger boxes for support and sat down on the sack of cloth. Where were they going?

The rhythmic motion of the oxcart combined with the heat of the sun beating down on her chador made Marta drowsy. She would have loved to pull the veil off her face and shake her hair in the wind. How wonderful it would feel to drink in the fresh air as they trundled down the road. But she dared not do it. It wasn't that Idris would see. After all, there was a barrier of packed goods between them, and Idris was facing away from her. But other people on the road could see her. What good Turkish woman would be seen unveiled? Marta couldn't risk being recognized as an Armenian, not even by a casual passerby. So she suffered in the heat.

The streets of Aintab faded in the distance. At first the road was fairly busy with farmers bringing in wagons of fresh produce or walking with their goats. And soldiers. Always soldiers. Some of them were so ragged and thin that she wondered how they could fight.

After a while there were fewer farmers on the road. But the soldiers were always there.

Once, as Marta drowsed in the heat, she was startled awake by a terrible grinding noise. She looked up and saw an automobile in a cloud of dust a fair distance behind them. She watched in fascination as it got closer and then idled behind the oxcart for a moment. The driver wore a black uniform. When the oxcart pulled over to the side and let the automobile pass, Marta could see the passenger clearly through the backseat window. It was a man with a lamb's wool fez and a military coat with a high-necked collar. Marta gasped when she saw the signature bushy upturned mustache. Could this passenger be Enver Pasha himself? The resemblance was uncanny. Marta had only seen pictures of Talaat Pasha, Djemal Pasha, and Enver Pasha—the three leaders of the Young Turk Government. But the automobile flashed by too quickly. Maybe it was a dream.

The route seemed familiar. Marta knew by the position of the sun that they were traveling north. Could this be the road that led to Marash? As she drifted between awake and asleep, she remembered the last time she had been on this road, April 1915. The captain of the Young Turk Army in Marash had come right into the orphanage compound and ordered all of the older orphans deported.

How many had walked down this road with her? How many had died on the side of this road—starved or clubbed to death with the butt of a rifle if they couldn't keep up?

Marta stifled a sob and sat up, fully awake. She rearranged the sacks and crates so that she was sitting at the edge of the cart. She propped the bag of cloth up onto the wooden ledge as a sort of pillow, then stretched her arms over the side, catching some breeze. When she looked down, she could see the dusty blur of the rock-strewn road below her.

Once, the ox stopped and then maneuvered around something in the road. As they passed, Marta craned her neck to see what it was. She gasped. Human skeletons, dried and dusty and crushed from many wagons. The jawbone of a skull and an intact spine were clearly visible. Marta shuddered. Were these the bones of Armenians from last year, or were they newer than that? What kind of country allowed human remains to be left on the roads?

She squeezed her eyes shut to banish the sight. The sun beat down on her black chador, making her feel like she was in the desert again. A memory burst to the surface—a bedraggled column of deportees marching into the heart of the desert. Thousands upon thousands of men, women, and children, half starved, with blistered feet and open sores showing through their rags.

Tears streamed down Marta's face, which made her veil cling uncomfortably. She had tried so hard to keep these thoughts away. They were just too painful to bear. Better not to think…

Hours later, the oxcart stopped. With a jolt, Marta sat up. She could hear the driver's boots on the gravel. She listened as he helped Idris down from the front bench of the cart.

A moment later, Marta saw the familiar kohl-lined eyes and furrowed brow framed by the black chador. The frown softened slightly at the sight of Marta's tear-swollen eyes. "We are spending the night here," said Idris gently. "Your name is Meral, and you're my daughter." Without waiting for an answer, she turned and walked away.

Marta stood up and stretched. Painstakingly she hoisted herself over the back of the cart, trying not to get her chador caught on the rough wood. She brushed off the loose bits of dust and straw.

The driver had unfastened his ox and was leading the animal to an enclosed courtyard.

"Your mistress is inside," he said, pointing to the door of a rustic country house.

Marta walked uncertainly up to the house and pushed open the door. Inside was a small entranceway with an uncovered door to the right. To the left, a curtain of beads hid another entrance. She pushed aside the long strings of beads and stepped in.

Idris had removed her chador, revealing her hair slick with sweat. She was sitting on a cushion on the floor in front of a low table. On the table sat a small earthen bowl of dried apricots and another of almonds.

"You can sit there," said Idris. She patted the pillow beside her.

Marta sat down. She didn't know what to do or say. Idris had been cold to her from the moment Marta had been granted refuge in her home. Marta knew that right now Idris was play-acting affection. It was obvious that she was trying to pass off Marta as a Turk. It was understandable. After all, any Turk caught hiding an Armenian would be killed and their house burnt to the ground. Nonetheless, it felt strange to be sitting beside her nemesis as if they were friends—no, more than that. Mother and daughter!

Just then, a plump young woman entered from a back room. Her hair was arranged in a single braid down her back, and she was dressed in the standard colorful tunic and trousers of a Turkish housewife. She carried a tray laden with ample quantities of simple peasant food.

"Kamelya *Hanim* (Mrs.)," said Idris to the innkeeper's wife. "This is my daughter, Meral."

"Allah is great," said Kamelya. "He has blessed you with a beautiful girl. Not too fatty. She will attract a rich husband."

Marta could feel Idris stiffen beside her. "Yes," replied Idris, after a momentary silence. "I have much to be thankful for."

Kamelya knelt down beside the low table, carefully balancing the tray as she did so. Then she transferred the items one by one onto the table. Marta's stomach growled at the tantalizing aroma of sliced cold lamb as it was set gently down. Then came small wild cucumbers, black olives, pungent cheeses, fresh flat bread, and tall glasses of *tan*, a yogurty drink that was one of Marta's favorites.

"We have other travelers who will be arriving later tonight," said Kamelya. "But of course you are the only women. When you are finished eating, please make yourself comfortable in the sleeping quarters." She motioned with her hand toward an alcove lined with cushions on the other side of the room. Then she left.

Idris and Marta ate in silence. Marta still had no idea why they were on this trip and where they were going. And she was afraid to ask.

Finally Idris said, "You are with child."

It wasn't a question. It was a statement.

"Y-yes," replied Marta.

Idris reached over and rested her palm on Marta's belly. It was barely rounded. But seven months ago it had been concave. A year ago, she had been a walking skeleton.

"You are with child," said Idris. "This is why you must leave."

Marta blinked with confusion. Conflicting emotions raced through her mind. "But this is what you wanted," she said in as even a voice as she could manage. The fact of her pregnancy was one of the many things that Marta had forced herself not to think about. She had been living hour to hour, day to day, not thinking of the future. She had not let herself think about the reality of this child. It was simply too painful.

"I thought I did want this child," said Idris in a strangled voice. "But if you give birth to a son, then you will be First Wife. I thought I could bear that, but now I realize that I would rather die."

For all the husband's brutishness, Marta knew how much Idris loved him. How it must have hurt her when he brought his second wife home. And how much had Marta's arrival hurt both the wives? She could only imagine. But what did Idris have in store for her? Where was she being taken and what would happen to this baby?

"I...I am grateful for all that you have done for me," said Marta. And she meant it. Idris could have turned her out at any time. Some days, Marta wished that Idris had done just that. Her life was difficult, but anything was better than the deportations— even the husband's nightly rapes. And she clung to the hope that Kevork still lived. If she died, what would become of him? She needed to live—not for herself but for him. And Marta had willingly paid the price. But what of this baby?

"Where are we going?" asked Marta.

"You realize that I could have just wrung your neck and been done with it?" said Idris coldly.

Marta gasped. Yes, it had been a constant fear. She dared not reply.

"I'm taking you back to the Germans," said Idris, "to that orphanage you always talk about."

Marta's heart nearly burst with excitement. "The orphanage is still there?" she asked.

"My sister says that it is," said Idris. "Although it is nearly empty."

"You have a sister in Marash?" asked Marta.

"Yes," said Idris. "She is with child and needs help with the birth. Adila will tell my husband that you have run off. Before I go to my sister's home, I will take you to the Germans."

All the emotions that Marta had tried to hold in for so long rushed to the surface. "Thank you!" she said. She embraced Idris with all her might. Tears streamed down her face.

Idris seemed to be at a loss. At first she tried to push Marta off, but then she gathered the younger woman in her arms and comforted her, almost as if Marta were really her daughter.

Three

KEVORK

Kevork threw his rucksack over one shoulder. He made his way past the crowded bazaar stalls, stopping once to buy some oranges. Then he walked out to the street and breathed in deeply. He welcomed the fresh breeze as it hit his face. Just ahead of him, high on the hill, was the Citadel—a centuries-old Arab fort with towers rising above a moat. He headed in the direction of the Citadel to the winding streets in the old part of Aleppo, where the houses were packed tightly against one another.

The narrow streets were bustling with activity. Most of the people who passed him were men—Arabs who wore the *gambaz* (long shirt) just as he did. They took no notice of him. He passed three Turkish soldiers. They didn't give him a second glance either. Maybe I haven't been found out then, thought Kevork as he pushed open the heavy wooden door to his dwelling.

The place was much larger than it appeared from the outside. The plaster walls were gray with grime and the dirt floor could barely be seen for the six huge, square wooden carpet looms, all buzzing with activity. There was not a stick of furniture or decorations anywhere, save for the gorgeous designs emerging from the looms themselves. Each loom held a distinctive carpet pattern, and behind each loom was a young Armenian girl. They each sat on the dirt floor, but a hole had been dug in the floor for

16

each of them so they could sit upright rather than cross-legged.

As Kevork stepped in, the weaving shuttles momentarily paused.

"It's just Kevork," said one of the girls. And they continued with their work.

When Kevork had first arrived in Aleppo, he'd taken refuge in an Armenian church. The priest had brought him to this place. The six young girls were already living there. They had survived the deportations because of their weaving skills. An Arab merchant had purchased the girls and set them up in this house. They lived much better than most of the orphaned children in Aleppo. They all ate and slept in the one room and rarely went out for fear of being identified.

Kevork knew that the priest had placed other Armenian survivors in various dwellings all over Aleppo. Missionaries helped the survivors too. But Kevork also knew from experience that the Turkish Army could sweep down at any time and grab whatever Armenians they could find. And with the current feeling of unrest in the air, it was not a comfortable way to live. And that's why he preferred to be known as Khedive Ayakkabici—Khedive the shoemaker—rather than Kevork Adomian, the deportee.

As Kevork snaked his way around the looms, he handed each girl an orange. The last loom held the distinctive beginnings of a single large sunburst design in the middle. The last carpet was also the only one woven in shades of green with yellow and white, and flecks of blue. The others were woven with the more standard red with black and blue.

When he reached the last loom, Kevork paused.

"How are you doing today, Angele?" he asked.

The little girl looked up at him and grinned. At age eleven, Angele was the youngest and most gifted of the six—and by far the most damaged. Her hands were a mass of scars from working the looms all day. And she was so skinny that her shoulder blades were clearly visible beneath the old flour sack that she had fashioned into a simple robe. Kevork liked to joke with her and say that her shoulder blades were her angel wings and that's how she got her name.

"I'm fine," she said, "but my hands are sore." Then she shrugged. "Nothing new about that."

Kevork's heart ached for all of the girls but especially for Angele. Maybe it was because during the Adana Massacre of 1909, he had lost Arsho. Angele was so like his little sister. Had Arsho lived, she would have been a carpet weaver too, just as Kevork's mother had been. There was a look of vulnerability in Angele's eyes that touched Kevork's heart. It was the same look that he had seen in Marta's eyes. Kevork wondered if Marta was surviving in a place like this, having the bleakness of her days brightened by someone bringing her an orange. Kevork hoped that strangers were kind to Marta. He prayed that she was still alive.

Kevork playfully tugged on a lock of Angele's hair. She grinned back before returning to her work.

Kevork stepped past her and climbed a set of earthen steps along the side of the room. The roof of the building was the place he called home. He glanced around at the sum of his existence. His bedding was still airing in the sunlight to keep away lice. A rugged lean-to provided shelter when it rained. A small gas burner was set up in one corner on a makeshift table. And two tin cans, which had been fashioned into cups, sat neatly inside a pot.

Kevork sat down at the table and emptied his pockets. He picked up the wedding ring and held it close to his face, looking at every scratch and mark of wear. The ring had been placed on a woman's hand in love; he wondered if it had been torn off in hate.

Or maybe it had been reluctantly taken off and exchanged for a bit of bread? He would never know. The ring fit his baby finger.

"If you are alive, Marta," he whispered, "I will find you. And with this ring, I will make you my wife."

Later that evening Angele stilled her loom and climbed up to the roof to visit with Kevork. As he boiled water for tea, she pointed to the ring on his finger. "Where did you get that?" she asked.

He told her of the soldier whose strap he had fixed.

"Does he know you're Armenian?" she asked, her eyes wide with fear.

"I'm not sure," said Kevork. He knew that if they found out about him, it wouldn't be long before Angele and the girls were also discovered. "Maybe I should move out."

"Let's not think about that right now," said Angele.

"We're all going to have to think about it soon," said Kevork. "Something's happening with the war and I don't know what, but the Turks are as mad as a swarm of bees." He set her cup on the table in front of her and then sat down beside her. He took Angele's damaged hands into his own, hoping that his warmth would ease some of her pain. They sat quietly together, listening to the crickets in the moonlight.

He tried not to think about the future.

Four

ZEKI

The boy watched from his hiding place in the doorstep as Vartan and a soldier with a brown rifle strap walked by. Noiselessly the boy followed them. He could overhear some of what they said. "Hiding, here...gold..." And it was enough that the boy knew he had to find the truth.

As he followed them into the poorest streets of Aleppo, the boy crinkled his nose at the foul smell. His father wouldn't be happy to see his son walking these streets. His father was the only Turkish surgeon in town and he was fanatical about cleanliness. How many times had he told the boy, "Bad smells mean germs, so stay away"?

But the boy couldn't stay away this time. He had to find out what Vartan was up to. Vartan was an Armenian courier working with the missionaries. Why would he be walking and talking with a Turkish soldier? Hadn't Vartan himself narrowly escaped the deportation marches? What was he thinking?

Vartan and the soldier stopped talking. As they turned around, the boy ducked behind a corner and held his breath. When he peeked out again, he was relieved to see that they had continued on their way. They hadn't noticed him.

Down some more winding roads. The smell got worse. Finally they stopped at a tumbledown inn. Vartan pointed to the building. The soldier nodded and pushed the door open. When he came out again, he was holding a cloth to his nose in disgust. Then he pulled out a fistful of bills from his pocket and shoved them at Vartan. The Armenian took the money, counted it quickly, and put the wad of bills into his own pocket. He nodded once to the soldier, then left. A few minutes later, the soldier also walked away.

The boy waited in his hiding place for one minute, then two. He poked his head out around the corner. Vartan was long gone. So was the soldier. The boy walked up to the inn and pushed the door open. The odor was so overpowering that vomit rose in his throat. Dozens of eyes latched onto his sorrowfully. Then the hands came out. "Please, water!" or "A bit of bread for my baby."

The room was filled with sick and emaciated Armenians, but the boy had nothing to give. He had seen places like this before. He shut the door and ran out into the street, his stomach churning not only from the smell but also with anger. Why had Vartan given away their hiding place?

The boy doubled over and vomited his lunch into the dusty outline of Vartan's footprints.

Five

JOHN COREN

He stepped into the entrance of the restaurant and surveyed the room. Amelia Schultz's familiar shock of red hair pulled unattractively back in a severe bun was nowhere to be seen. Most of the tables were empty, although one was occupied by a fat Turkish businessman smoking a cigar. An untouched demitasse of coffee sat in front of him, and he drummed his fingers impatiently on the table.

When John Coren walked past his table, the man looked up expectantly and then lowered his eyes in disappointment. John brushed past another table where two fashionably dressed German women talked animatedly about something unimportant. They nibbled on cucumber sandwiches and sipped their tea. They didn't notice him.

John sat down at his usual table in the darkened far corner. All of the tables around him were empty.

"A whiskey," he said to the waiter who appeared instantly at his side. "Be quick with it," he added. "And when the lady comes, bring us tea with lemon."

As the waiter hurried away, John opened his newspaper and tried to read, but the words swam before his eyes. Why had Amelia called him so urgently? It couldn't be good news. He brushed his hand over the lapel of his jacket and felt the thick ridge of the envelope that was tucked just inside his jacket. At least this new money from America had arrived and he would be able to give it to Amelia now. He hoped that this would be enough money to tide her over.

The waiter brought a small tumbler of whiskey and John downed it in a single gulp before handing it back to the waiter. And just as he looked up, he could see the familiar silhouette of Amelia standing in the doorway. "Bring the tea," said John to the waiter. Then he stood up and waved so that Amelia could see him.

"Sorry I'm late," she said breathlessly, untying the head scarf that covered her bright red hair, then folding it neatly and stuffing it into her satchel.

"I just got here myself," said John. "What has happened now?"

Amelia leaned back against her chair. Then, pretending to fuss with her skirt, she looked from left to right to see if anyone was in hearing distance. The waiter approached with a pot of tea, china cups and saucers, and a bowl of lemon wedges.

"Lovely, John," she said, a wide grin pasted on her face. "This tea will hit the spot."

Once the waiter moved away, she leaned forward to pour tea for them both. She handed him his cup and whispered, "Another group of our deportees has been caught."

John Coren set the delicate teacup down on its saucer with a clatter. He stared angrily at Amelia. "It can't possibly have happened again," he said.

"It did," she replied, gripping her own teacup to hide the trembling in her hands.

"Do you know who turned them in?" asked John.

"I...I...think it was Vartan," said Amelia.

John leaned slowly back in his chair and attempted to hide his shock. Vartan Onnissian was an Armenian deportee. Like so many others, he had lost his whole family but had somehow managed to survive. In a red fez and expensive tailored suit, he looked every bit the Turkish businessman. He was one of their most trusted underground couriers.

"It can't be," said John. "Why would he harm other Armenians?"

"Cash," said Amelia simply. "The last I gave him never got to its destination."

John suppressed a groan of frustration.

"Plus the police have been paying him one Turkish pound for every Armenian he identifies."

"How did you find out?" asked John.

"Zeki followed him," said Amelia.

Six

MARTA

Marta woke up early the next morning, excited and fearful at the same time. The orphanage in Marash was the only place left that she could possibly call home. Would they, *could* they, take her in?

It was an hour before sunset prayer when the oxcart finally rolled through the streets of Marash. Marta peered over the crates in the back of the cart, trying to drink in all of the familiar sights and smells.

But while the aroma of coffee and spices and baking bread were familiar, something else was not. The pervading odor of something rotten. Marash had always been a city of cultural richness, with Christians, Muslims, and Jews living side by side in relative peace. But now the streets were mostly filled with men wearing fezzes and women wearing chadors.

The oxcart turned and headed down a familiar street. Marta caught her breath as she saw a group of women gathered around the communal baking pit in the central courtyard. The weekly baking of the *lavosh* (Armenian cracker bread) had been as much a party as a chore, and Marta had fond memories of going there with her grandmother. But now, all of the women were veiled and spoke Turkish. As the cart got closer, Marta heard a familiar laugh. Could it be Mariam?

Marta tried to push herself up to get a better view, but all that was visible in the sea of black veils were the women's eyes and hands. Her older sister could be there and Marta would never know it. The cart passed so close that Marta could have reached out and touched the woman with the laugh. She peered into her eyes. Not Mariam. Marta swallowed a sob of disappointment.

The cart continued down the street. They passed a lone ragged boy sitting cross-legged on the side of the road, his hand extended in a plea for coins. He looked the same age as Onnig. Was her brother still alive? Was he begging on another street somewhere too? Or was he living a life of ease as the adopted son of a Turkish family? It was another possibility that Marta didn't want to think about.

And then they passed the house where her grandmother had lived until last year. Marta wished she could jump out of the cart, push open the familiar gate, and run into her grandmother's arms again. But it was impossible to turn back the clock. Her grandmother was dead.

Just then a man dressed in wide Turkish pants and a fez stepped out from the front doorway and began to pick figs from her grandmother's tree in the courtyard. The sight made her stomach churn. It was as if her grandmother had never existed.

The oxcart continued on to a busy thoroughfare. Here, soldiers were milling about. Elderly beggars dressed in rags lay propped up against doorsteps. Bone-thin street urchins stared up at her from their makeshift hovels behind stoops. Some of the urchins were begging, but it was the rare adult who gave up a coin or a bit of bread. Once, when the wagon paused to make way for an automobile, a child came right up to Marta, filthy hand outstretched and round eyes pleading. But Marta had nothing to give.

In the crowds of adults milling about, Marta could see mostly Turks and a few Kurds and Arabs, but not a single identifiable

Armenian. If they existed, they were hidden, or disguised as she was.

Finally the oxcart stopped. They were at the orphanage. Marta stared up at the tall stone walls.

Four Turkish soldiers with bayonets guarded the gate. Marta didn't know whether she was supposed to hide or to sit up straight in the back of the cart, like a good Turkish servant. She decided to sit up straight.

One of the soldiers approached the ox-driver. "What's your business here?" he asked.

"My mistress, Idris Hanim," said the driver, gesturing toward his seatmate with a jerk of his head. "She wants to see the person in charge."

"About what?" asked the soldier, turning his attention to Idris.

"I am looking for a son," she said.

The soldier nodded. Many Turkish families came to the orphanage to adopt Armenian waifs and bring them up in the true religion. "There aren't many left," he said, "but go ahead."

"Open the gates," he called to the other soldiers.

When the gates closed behind them and Marta was on the other side, she expected to feel exhilarated. But instead she felt bereft. The courtyard was empty and still. As the cart rolled to a stop in front of the main office, she wondered if Miss Younger, the German missionary who had supervised the orphanage in 1915, was still there.

Idris walked around to the back of the cart. She too looked surprised at the emptiness of the orphanage. She wouldn't be taking a son home from here.

"Let me help you down," she said, reaching her hand in and grasping Marta's firmly.

Marta was struck by her demeanor. At the inn, Marta thought she was feigning affection, but there was no need for duplicity here. Did this mean that Idris was actually starting to miss her? More than likely, it was all the housecleaning Idris would miss. No, Marta thought again, that was being unfair. Idris did not have to go through so much trouble to get rid of her. Marta owed this woman her life.

The driver waited while Idris and Marta stood at Miss Younger's door. Marta turned to Idris and held out her hand. "Thank you," she said.

Idris grasped her hand and kissed Marta on both cheeks. "Allah is good," she said. "May you have a happy life."

Idris didn't wait for Marta to knock on the door. She walked back to the oxcart and climbed up. "Take me to my sister's," she said to the driver.

Marta watched the cart roll back through the gates. She had a moment of panic. What if the soldiers threw her out? But they didn't seem to notice her. The gates closed and she was hidden from the outside world. Marta pulled off her chador and draped it over one arm. She held her face up to the sky and breathed in deeply.

She lifted her hand and gave the door a sharp rap.

There was no answer at the orphanage administrator's door. She rapped again and waited. No answer.

She turned the knob. It was open. She stepped inside. The office had been recently used. An empty cup sat on the desk with the dregs of coffee still wet at the bottom, and papers with that day's date were strewn across the surface. An odd black machine with a handle and wires sat on the corner of the desk. Marta had heard of telephones and telegraphs—machines that made instant communication possible through wires. But she had never seen one. She dared not touch it.

Marta stepped out and shut the door behind her. She walked into the middle of the empty courtyard. What if Miss Younger had left? What if there was nobody here? She had a moment of panic. But she took a deep calming breath. There *had* to be someone there.

One end of the compound had housed the girls' orphanage, known as *Bethel*. The boys' orphanage, called *Beitshalom*, sat on the other side of the grounds. The orphanage complex was like a city within a city. There had to be at least one other person here.

As Marta walked through Bethel, she remembered the first time she had arrived and how amazed she'd been at the sheer number of windows. Most of the buildings were constructed like army barracks—brick and wood and cement. There was a pharmacy, a church, the school, administrative buildings, houses for the missionaries and teachers, and the dormitories.

Back then, the orphanage had hummed with activity: singing, laughing, bobbins spinning noisily through the shuttles of weaving looms. Then there were the everyday sounds of a classroom, with papers rustling, a teacher's voice droning on. Marta still remembered the aroma of freshly baking bread and the whiff of hot clean dampness coming from the laundry as she had passed by.

She looked out at the vast courtyard and remembered it filled with laughing and playing children. She walked out into the center of the courtyard, closed her eyes, and remembered the last time she had stood in this exact same spot. Was it just a year ago? So much had happened since then.

✣

They had been ordered to pack their clothing and bedrolls. They sat in uneasy rows in the courtyard. Most of the children were under the age of twelve and were not slated for deportation. But Marta, her sister Mariam, and her beloved Kevork had all been in their mid-teens. They knew they might be discovered amongst the children and deported.

Their one hope was to stay together. Marta had borrowed a man's pair of trousers and shirt. Kevork had cut off all her hair. It was safer to be seen as a boy. But Mariam had refused. What good would it have done? Mariam's delicate figure would have never passed for male.

⚜

A tear trickled out of one corner of Marta's closed eyes as she imagined herself sitting on her bedroll, Mariam on one side and Kevork on the other, the children behind them. She thought of poor dear Paris, the child with the mischievous eyes, and of Parantzim, the orphan rescued just the day before the inspection.

⚜

Miss Younger and the missionaries stood to one side. Beside them stood the only adult Armenians in the complex—Aunt Anna, Mr. Karellian, the boys' trade teacher, and Tante (Aunt) Maria, the elderly laundress.

Suddenly the massive gates creaked open and an officer on a white stallion sauntered in, followed by soldiers on foot. He reined his horse inches from Miss Younger's face and glanced from her to the other adults. "Where are your adult Armenians?" he asked, cracking his whip toward the sorry group.

"These three are all who live here," said Miss Younger.

The rows of children just meters away were so fearful that not a single child took a breath.

"The records show that you have a dozen Armenians on staff."

"The records are mistaken," replied Miss Younger.

The officer dismounted. He walked over to the children, who sat in silence.

He stopped in front of Kevork and stared down at the young

30

man as he sat quietly on his bedroll. Crooking his finger, he beckoned Kevork to stand. Kevork blushed, then obliged. He was a
head taller than the officer.

"This is no child." And then with a motion of his finger, the
officer directed Kevork to join the adult Armenians.

"He's only fifteen!" cried Miss Younger.

"I don't believe you," replied the officer.

Next, he stepped in front of Marta. Her heart pounded
wildly.

As he did with Kevork, he ordered her to stand. She would
have towered over him, but she crouched slightly. "Here is another
man," he said angrily.

"That…boy…" Miss Younger stumbled. "That boy is only
thirteen. He's no risk to you."

"If these are children, then you're feeding them too well." He
gestured to Marta to stand with Kevork and the adults. At least
they weren't separated.

When the officer stepped in front of Mariam, his face broke
into a smile. Brushing the side of her cheek lightly with his hand,
he turned to Miss Younger. "Where have you been hiding this
one?"

Miss Younger's face flushed, but she remained silent.

He grabbed Mariam's hand and pulled her toward him.
"You will come with me."

She stepped back. "No," she said. "I would rather be deported."

He shrugged, then casually drew a pistol from his belt. He
shot Paris, the little girl with the mischievous eyes. Blood splat-
tered from the wound in her neck as she fell back into the arms of
the girl sitting behind her. Miss Younger stepped forward, intend-
ing to help the injured girl, but the officer pointed his pistol and
asked, "Do you want to be next?"

Paris died before their eyes, but the children surrounding her maintained their grim silence. They watched as the officer inspected the rest of the children and designated about a dozen in all as "adults."

"I will be back for these adult Armenians at dawn tomorrow," the officer said. Then he walked to where Mariam stood and grabbed her by the hand. "They will die, but you will live."

He pushed Mariam onto his horse, then mounted in front of her, and with the soldiers following on foot, he left the compound.

It was the last time Marta would see her sister. The next morning she, Kevork, and the other "adults" began their death march into the desert.

><<>

Marta sighed deeply. So many bad memories. She opened her eyes and looked at the emptiness of the courtyard. Surely someone else was here?

Marta walked to one of the classroom buildings and pushed open the door. She gasped. The furniture was gone. She walked to the next building and the next. It was all the same. Furniture and supplies were sparse or nonexistent.

She pushed open the door to the kitchen and started. An elderly Armenian woman stood at a counter with her arms up to the elbow in dough.

"My God!" cried the old woman, putting one flour-covered hand to her heart. "Why did you scare me like that?" Then the woman squinted and stared at Marta, puzzled. "Who are you?"

"I...I...My name is Marta Hovsepian." Marta's heart was pounding so hard that she could hardly get the words out. "I was an orphan here."

"Before the deportations, you mean?" said the old woman, wiping her hands with a towel and brushing off the front of her apron. She extended one hand to Marta and said, "You can call me Sarah *Baji* (Grandmother)."

Marta reached out and took the warm, paper-thin hand in her own. Then, on impulse, she folded the woman into her arms. Sarah Baji was dovelike in her fragility and only came up to Marta's chin. She was nothing physically like Anahid Baji, Marta's own grandmother, but embracing the old woman brought a rush of tears to Marta's eyes.

"I know, I know," said Sarah Baji, patting Marta gently on the back as if she were comforting a child. "But you are safe now, so let us think of that."

Marta took a deep shuddering breath and tried to compose herself. "Are you the only one here?" she asked.

Sarah Baji held Marta at arm's length. Her eyes sparkled with amusement. "No, my dear. If I were the only one, would I be making all this food?"

Marta looked around. In addition to the giant bowl of bread dough, onions filled a wooden bowl and eggplants sat on the counter in front of the bowl. A huge vat of broth simmered on the stove.

"Where is everyone?" asked Marta.

"The little ones who were here at the time of the deportations are all gone now," said Sarah Baji.

"Were they deported too?" asked Marta.

"Some were," replied the old woman. "But most were adopted by Turkish families. Others were taken to a Turkish orphanage to be raised as Turks."

Marta nodded. Of course. What had she expected? At least the children were alive. Perhaps some day they would be brought back to the orphanage and relearn Armenian ways. But it sickened her to think that in the meantime, children whose parents had been killed by Turks were being raised to hate Armenians.

"Are there no children here at all, then?" asked Marta.

"A few have trickled back," said Sarah Baji. She took Marta by the hand and led her out the door and down to one of the classrooms.

Wooden benches and chairs filled the room. Only a few rows were occupied. Marta counted ten very young girls and two young boys. They were all dressed in simple straight shifts of unbleached cotton. Marta was relieved to see that the children appeared clean and fed. They looked up at her in curiosity and then quickly went back to their work.

A woman sat at a wooden desk at the front of the classroom. She was dressed in a long black skirt and white blouse with her gray hair caught up in a bun, and her head, a pen behind one ear, was bent over a ledger. She glanced briefly at the visitor but seemed to take no interest. A moment passed.

The woman looked up again. Abruptly she stood up, nearly knocking her ledger to the floor.

"Can that be you, Marta Hovsepian?" she asked.

Marta was equally taken aback. It was Miss Younger. Older, careworn, and distracted, but unmistakably Miss Younger. She walked up to Marta and reached out to touch her cheek. "Thank God that you have survived," she said.

Marta wrapped her arms around Miss Younger and gently rested her head on the older woman's shoulder, breathing in the familiar scent of soap, sweat, and talcum powder.

Miss Younger held Marta an arm's length away and looked her in the eyes. Then her gaze fell to Marta's abdomen. She turned to the students, who were watching the scene unfold before them.

"You are dismissed," she said.

They folded their books shut and filed out of the room.

Seven

KEVORK

Kevork put both pairs of sturdy walking boots into his satchel yet again. He walked down the familiar winding streets, but when he got to the market, he could see a group of Turkish soldiers milling about. That decided it. He walked on.

In about ten minutes he stopped. On the other side of the road sat a massive stone building surrounded by an ornate metal gate painted a gleaming black. Two Turkish guards stood in the doorway. This was the American consulate of Aleppo. Kevork watched for a few minutes, hoping that maybe the American who had ordered the boots would step out. But no one appeared.

Kevork crossed the street. He walked past the consulate once, looking at the guards through the corner of his eye. They ignored him. He turned around and walked past again. This time one of the guards stepped in front of him, blocking his way. Normally, having a Turkish guard accost him in this way would have sent shivers of apprehension through him. But this guard seemed somehow inoffensive. It could have had something to do with the fact that he looked still too young to shave. Or maybe it was the crumbs of bread scattered on the front of his uniform.

"Do you have business here?" asked the guard in Arabic.

"An American ordered boots from me and he hasn't paid," Kevork lied.

"What American?" asked the guard.

Kevork hesitated. The American had given him a name. He set his satchel down and rummaged through until he found the pouch that held his stack of receipts. He flipped through and pulled out the one he was looking for.

"Davis," he said. "Leslie Davis."

"He is not from the consulate," said the guard.

Kevork frowned in confusion. "He said he was a consul."

"Maybe for a city in Turkey," said the guard. "Mr. Jackson is the consul for Aleppo, and he has no one working in Syria by the name of Davis."

"Thank you," said Kevork, picking up his satchel.

As he began to walk away, the other guard said, "The place to find Americans is at the Baron Hotel. Maybe your Mr. Davis is there."

Kevork brightened. "Thank you!"

"The hotel is just down that way," pointed the guard.

Kevork followed the guard's directions until he arrived at a huge two-story stone building. This was the Baron Hotel and it was barely a decade old. Kevork could understand why rich foreigners stayed here when they came to Aleppo, as it was certainly clean and spacious. Kevork stood there for a few moments. The doorman was dressed in a red velvet outfit that could only be described as a costume. He held the door open and two women stepped out. Kevork couldn't tell if they were American or German or some other western nationality. Neither had covered her face nor even her hair, but they each opened up a parasol to protect themselves from the sun. Were these diplomats' wives? Their dresses were too fancy for missionaries. He marveled at the fact that they were free to walk in relative safety in what for them was a foreign country and a war-torn one at that. Yet here he was, an Armenian born just across the border in Turkey, and he didn't have the same freedom.

Kevork brushed the dirt from his robes and wiped the sweat from his face with the end of his sleeve. He walked up to the Baron Hotel. The doorman stepped in front of the entrance protectively and regarded Kevork with a disdainful look.

"May I help you?" he said.

"I am looking for an American," said Kevork.

The doorman smirked. "Any American in particular?"

"Davis," he said. "Leslie Davis."

The doorman's face changed at the sound of the name. "Go right in," he said, holding the door open.

As he stepped inside, Kevork caught his breath in wonder. This place was so different from anything he had ever seen before—so open and luxurious. A faint scent of fresh lemon hung in the air. The floor was covered with a sumptuous Turkish carpet with a vibrant swirling pattern in deep red, blue, and gold. The dark wood-paneled walls were inlaid with green, beige, and brown tiles. A huge crystal chandelier was suspended from the center of the vaulted ceiling.

Kevork walked up to a polished counter where a man with a monocle was busy scribbling something into a ledger. Behind the man was a vast honeycomb of cubbyholes, each one filled with a key on a small numbered stick. Kevork stood in front of the counter, but the man didn't look up. He wrinkled his nose as if he could smell something bad but continued to write in his ledger.

Finally Kevork cleared his throat with a loud, "Ahem."

The desk clerk looked up. In perfect Arabic, he said, "Is there something I can do for you?"

"I am here to see an American," said Kevork. "His name is Leslie Davis."

The clerk's eyes widened with recognition at the name. "You don't have an appointment," he stated. Then he continued with his work.

So the American *was* here! If he had been here all along, why had he not come back to get his walking boots? And why weren't they both on their way to Marash right now?

"I do have an appointment with him," said Kevork, trying for bravado. "He is expecting me this morning."

The desk clerk regarded Kevork with a look of pitying disdain. "Somehow I don't think so," he said. "You may as well leave."

"I am not going to leave until I see Mr. Davis," replied Kevork.

"Then you're going to be waiting an awfully long time," said the clerk.

✲

Kevork luxuriated at the high-backed red leather chair that enveloped him. Never in his life had he experienced a chair this comfortable. His stomach grumbled with hunger as the delicate aroma of cinnamon and freshly ground coffee wafted from the dining room. But he didn't move. He had been sitting in this chair in the lobby for nearly three hours. What he would give for a cup of water. But then again, if he had water, he'd have to relieve himself, and the whole point of sitting here was to pressure the desk clerk into letting him see Leslie Davis. Either that, or wait until Mr. Davis happened into the lobby himself. The American wouldn't stay in his room all day, would he?

It had turned out to be an educational experience, sitting and watching the various people strolling through the lobby. Kevork assumed that the people coming in were mostly American, although many were German. Kevork had heard gossip in the market that all sorts of foreigners were here, but the British,

Americans, Canadians, and Germans all looked alike to Kevork. How could the men stand to wear those hot black woolen suits in the heat? And why didn't the women realize that covering their heads with a light silk veil would provide more sun protection than those silly parasols?

The desk clerk glanced up every once in a while, and when he saw Kevork still sitting there, an expression—as if he had bitten into a rotten egg—would cross his face. Once, the doorman approached Kevork and asked him to leave. Kevork calmly shook his head.

Just when Kevork thought he would fall asleep if he sat there any longer, a porter approached him. "You are looking for Leslie Davis?"

Kevork nodded.

"Come with me."

Kevork followed the man up a wide set of marble steps and along a tapestry-filled hallway. He walked up to Room 202 and tapped lightly. From inside, a man's voice said, "Let him in."

The porter took a key from a collection on his belt and opened up the room. He motioned with his hand for Kevork to step in. Then the porter left.

The room was as impressive as the lobby but on a smaller scale. As his feet sank into the thick red carpet, the sun shone through a huge arched window and made the chandelier glitter like diamonds. Beneath the chandelier was a dining table with chairs for six. In the center of the table sat a silver tray and a bowl of fruit, olives, flat bread, and *böregi*—cigar-sized tubes of pastry wrapped around aromatic cheese and parsley. The tray also held several crystal glasses and a decanter filled with amber liquid. A dark-haired foreigner sat at the table.

It was not Leslie Davis.

"Sit," said the man, indicating with a flick of his hand the dining chair across from his own.

Kevork did as he was told, placing his rucksack by his feet. The delicate aroma of the böregi made his stomach grumble.

"Who are you?" asked the man.

"I am Khedive Ayakkabici," Kevork replied.

"Why are you here?" the foreigner asked in Arabic.

"To see Leslie Davis," said Kevork.

"How do you know about Leslie Davis?" asked the man, his eyes fixed on Kevork's face.

Kevork bent to open his rucksack. The man stiffened, but when Kevork drew out the walking boots, his shoulders relaxed. "He ordered these from me," said Kevork. "But then he never came back to pick them up."

"If it's payment you want," said the man, "I can look after that." He took out a billfold and began to count out money.

"No," said Kevork. "I have been paid."

"Then what do you want?"

Kevork regarded the man. Should he tell him? What was the worst the man could do to him? "We were going to go north together, back to Turkey."

The man gave a sharp intake of breath. "Why would you want to do that?"

"I am from Marash, and..." Kevork stopped mid-sentence. His heart felt like it was going to burst from his chest. The man had asked him the question in Armenian! And without thinking, Kevork had begun to answer him in Armenian as well.

The room was heavy with silence.

Then the man said, again in Armenian, "If you are an Armenian, then I am your friend."

Kevork said nothing. Was the man trying to trick him?

From the look on his face, it was obvious that the man knew what was running through Kevork's mind.

The man stood up. He undid his belt and dropped his pants to the floor.

The man was uncircumcised.

He wasn't a Muslim.

But what was he?

The man pulled his pants back up and said to Kevork, "If you're Armenian, prove it."

"My real name is Kevork Adomian," he said. "I was saved from the deportations by an Arab family in the desert. Before the deportations, I lived at the orphanage in Marash." Kevork began to undo his belt. "Would you like me to show you that I am uncircumcised?"

"It won't be necessary," said the man.

"Who are you?" asked Kevork.

"My Armenian name is Mgerdich Krekorian, but I'm an American, and I'm called John Coren. My parents immigrated to America and I was born in Boston," said the man. "I'm a missionary. I was stationed at the mission in Harput, and I knew Consul Davis well."

Kevork felt weak at the knees. He slumped back down into his chair. The American was *Armenian*? And why did he say he knew Mr. Davis? Did that mean Mr. Davis was dead?

"Drink this whiskey," said John, pouring two fingers' worth of the amber liquid into a crystal glass and pushing it across the table. "It will calm you down."

Kevork took a huge gulp and sputtered as the fiery liquid burned down his throat. It didn't make him calm. Instead, he felt immediately dizzy.

"Eat," said John, shoving the whole tray of food in front of Kevork.

Kevork grabbed a böregi and shoved it into his mouth, chasing away the burn of the whiskey. As he chewed, he tried to sort the situation out in his mind.

"Mr. Davis is alive," said John. "He is at the consulate in Harput."

Despite the fact that he barely knew the man, Kevork was glad that Leslie Davis was alive and safe.

"But we were going to travel north together."

"He had to leave earlier than expected," said John. "These are uncertain times, as you know."

Kevork was crushed by the news. How would he get back to Marash now? One needed travel documents, diplomatic immunity—items that were completely out of a poor Armenian's reach. It was impossible for him to travel alone through the heart of Turkey and back to the orphanage in Marash without being caught. He hoped that accompanying an important American like Leslie Davis would have provided him with safety. How would he get back now?

"You cannot go back there," said John, as if he had read Kevork's mind.

"I must," replied Kevork. "I promised my betrothed that if I survived, I would get back to the orphanage in Marash."

A wave of sorrow passed over John Coren's face. "What are the chances that your beloved survived?" he asked.

Kevork did not reply. It was something that he dared not think about. In fact, the thought of Marta somehow surviving was the only thing that kept him alive.

"You cannot travel back into the heart of Turkey," repeated John. "You will never make it alive."

Kevork took a deep breath and sighed. He nodded slowly. Maybe it was the whiskey, or maybe it was the realization that he couldn't travel alone to find Marta, but when Kevork stood to leave, his body felt so heavy and weak that his legs could barely take his weight.

"Where are you going?" asked John, looking surprised.

"Does it matter?" asked Kevork sadly.

"Sit down, young man," said John. "I have a proposition for you."

Kevork sat back down heavily and cradled his head in his arms. He really didn't care about this man's proposition. If he couldn't get back to Marta, what did it matter?

"You have the perfect disguise," said John.

"Perfect for what?" asked Kevork, not bothering to lift his head from his arms.

"To be our courier," said John. "This is an Arab town and you blend in perfectly. We need to get money to the Armenian safe houses in town, but the government is watching all of the missionaries."

Kevork lifted his head. He knew that there were many buildings all over Aleppo that served as hiding places for Armenians. He also knew that the people who hid there were in dire straits.

Another thought crossed his mind: what if Marta *hadn't* been able to return to Marash for the same reason that he couldn't? She could be hiding in Aleppo, in Aintab, or anywhere along the deportation routes.

"I'll do it," said Kevork. "But I have a favor to ask as well."

John regarded him intently. "What would that be?"

"You keep lists, don't you?" asked Kevork.

"You mean of the Armenians that we find alive?" responded John.

"Yes," said Kevork. "Those lists."

"You want me to tell you if your beloved shows up on one of these lists?" said John.

43

Kevork nodded.

"Write her name on this sheet of paper and I'll see what I can do," said John. "We will be in touch."

Kevork did as he was told. When he left, he wondered what he had got himself into.

Ⓜ

John Coren watched the door close behind Kevork and then sighed deeply. He looked down at the piece of paper with Marta's name on it. As far as he was concerned, the worst thing that could happen to Kevork would be for him to find the girl. John had seen some of the women who had survived—raped over and over, mutilated, and crazed from the experience. It was better for those women to die. At least that way their suffering would end and they would live on nobly in the memory of their loved ones.

And there was another issue that was more urgent. How long could he expect Kevork to help with the hidden deportees if Marta was found? John had seen it before: a reunion—never as happy as they thought it would be—and then extreme avoidance of risk. He desperately needed a courier and Kevork seemed perfect. He'd keep him wondering about Marta for as long as he could.

He reached over to the tray in the center of the table, grabbed a fresh crystal glass, and poured himself a generous two fingers of whiskey. He downed it in a single gulp and put the glass back down heavily on the table. He picked up the piece of paper again and held it up to his face.

"And what, pray tell, have they done to you, Marta Hovsepian?" he asked. "If you're still alive, do you wish that you were dead?

Eight

MARTA

After the last orphan filed out of the room, a worried look transformed Miss Younger's face. "Are you with child?"

"Yes," said Marta, her bottom lip trembling.

"Is Kevork the father?"

"No," said Marta.

"Do you know who the father is?" asked Miss Younger.

"Yes," said Marta. Then she explained how she had escaped from the deportations and how she had been rescued by Adila, the second wife. In halting words, she began to explain the rest.

"Hush," said Miss Younger softly, holding one finger to her lips. "There is no blame for you to feel and no need to explain." Then she wrapped her arms around Marta's shoulders and rocked her gently.

Marta sank into Miss Younger's embrace. "I am so frightened," said Marta. "I don't know what to do."

"There is time to think about this," said Miss Younger. "Come with me."

With one arm still wrapped around Marta's shoulder, Miss Younger took Marta through the orphanage compound. For Marta, it was like going back in time. She had spent so many happy days at Bethel. It was here that she had learned to read and write in both German and Armenian. She had learned a

45

smattering of English too. She had grown strong and healthy here and had learned to be self-sufficient. She had also fallen in love with Kevork here.

"You have many things to think about," said Miss Younger. "You need time for reflection. Time to sort out your own mind."

And then they were at a familiar door. Miss Younger pushed it open and they stepped inside. "This is your home, my dear," said Miss Younger. "Get some rest. We shall talk later." With that, Miss Younger left.

Marta stepped inside the room that used to be her old dormitory. Like most of the rooms at the orphanage, it had not been in use since the deportations. Dusty bedrolls leaned against the edge of the wall and the bare bed frames looked forlorn, like skeletons in a row. Marta lifted up one of the bedrolls and shook it out. She spread it over the bed frame that had been her own. She found sheets in the cupboard, clean but musty-smelling. She made her bed and lay down on it.

She closed her eyes and remembered the last time she had been in this room. So much had happened since then. She turned her head and stared at the empty bed beside her. That was where Mariam had slept. Would she ever see her sister again? Marta wiped away a tear with the back of her hand. She placed her hand on her belly. If Mariam was alive, was she pregnant too? Marta squeezed her eyes tight, as if to banish any more speculation. As her hand rested on her belly, she felt a quickening. For a moment she experienced pure joy. A baby—her own child—grew within her. A new life amidst all this death.

Kevork. If he lived, what would he think of her now? Would he turn away from her in disgust? And what would he think of the baby? How could he possibly love this child?

No matter how tightly she squeezed her eyes shut, tears

streamed down the sides of her face and into her hair. She took deep gulps of air, trying to keep back the sobs, but she had held them in for months. There was no one to listen to her here. Finally, she gave into her sorrow and wept and wept until she could weep no more.

><--†--><

She must have fallen asleep because when she opened her eyes, her room was dark. Only a bit of moonlight shone through the window. She pulled the covers up to her neck and shivered in the night air. What am I going to do about this baby? she thought. What can I do?

She wrapped the covers around her shoulders like a cape and then got out of bed. Without thinking about how she must look— wild hair streaming down her back, bare feet, and a Turkish housedress covered with a blanket—Marta walked out of the building and toward Miss Younger's office. But when she got there, she saw that no light was on. She turned around and began to walk back to her dormitory when she passed the kitchen. She could see a strip of light from underneath the door. She tapped lightly, in case it was Sarah Baji inside. She didn't want to frighten the old woman twice in one day. When no one answered, Marta pushed the door open.

Miss Younger and Sarah Baji both looked up, startled. They each had their hands wrapped around a steaming cup, and by their guilty glances Marta wondered if she had been the topic of conversation.

"Come and sit," said Sarah Baji, patting the wooden chair beside her.

Marta stepped in, grateful for the warmth of the kitchen but also for the invitation.

Sarah Baji stood up and walked over to the stove. It took only a moment to bring it back to a boil. She threw in an extra spoon-ful of tea leaves and added the boiling water to the teapot. She brought the pot and an extra cup and set it down in front of Marta.

Marta stared at the bits of steam rising from the tea spout as if she could find an answer to her dilemma there. One big tear rolled down the side of her face and plopped onto the wooden table.

"I cannot have this baby," she said.

Miss Younger and Sarah Baji exchanged glances but said nothing. Moments passed while Marta's declaration hung in the air. Sarah poured the freshly steeped tea into the waiting mug and slid the mug over to Marta.

"There are herbs that you can take," she said.

Surprised, Marta looked up at her and blinked. "Herbs?" she asked.

"Yes," said Sarah. "For times when it is inconvenient to have a child. The recipe has been passed down from mother to daughter for generations."

Marta hadn't had a mother since she was nine. She often won-dered how much her mother knew but never had time to tell her. What would her mother have suggested she do in her current sit-uation? She desperately did not want to have this baby.

"Do you know how to make this recipe?" asked Marta.

"I do," said Sarah Baji. "If you wish, I will prepare the herbs for you tomorrow."

Marta looked at Sarah Baji's face and tried to read the emo-tions she saw there—sorrow, determination, and sympathy. Then she looked at Miss Younger. On the older woman's face was only one emotion: distress.

"Do you not think I should do this?" Marta asked.

"You are far along in the pregnancy," said Miss Younger. "The herbs may not work."

Marta wrapped the blanket closer around her trembling shoulders. She reached down and rested the palm of her hand against the swelling in her abdomen. She felt a quickening again. Her heart leapt for joy, but almost immediately she was plunged back into despair.

"Sarah Baji, I would like you to prepare those herbs for me," she said.

Marta reached for her cup of tea and sipped it in silence. The other two women sipped their own tea but were silent too. Marta noticed Sarah Baji give Miss Younger a meaningful look. Miss Younger's response was a slight shake of her head. The exchange confused Marta. Was there something they weren't telling her? Neither would look her in the eye, so once she finished her tea, she got up to leave. "Thank you," she said as she walked out the door.

✦

Sarah Baji watched Marta close the door behind her and then turned to Miss Younger. "I thought you were going to tell her about her sister."

Miss Younger sighed. "Now is not the time."

Nine

ZEKI

Zeki Aygun sat cross-legged on the roof of his father's surgery and waited for Jujij, his rock dove, to fly down and sit on his shoulder. He knew that he had to be very still or his beloved bird wouldn't alight. Zeki had a handful of bread crumbs and a bowl of water at his side.

Zeki felt guilty about feeding Jujij. After all, there were so many people without food. But when Zeki first encountered the dove here on his father's roof, Jujij was frail from hunger and her wing had been broken. Zeki nursed her back to health and then watched in sorrow when she flew away. But then the next day, she came back. And the next, and the next day after that.

Zeki closed his eyes and breathed in and out slowly as he waited for Jujij to arrive. This was his favorite part of any day. It was so quiet up here; it gave him a chance to let his mind empty of all the disturbing things he had seen and done. How many twelve-year-olds disobeyed their government as he did? Who would stop a Turkish boy as he wandered from one street to another? How many times had he let Amelia tape money to his chest? Once he put his long shirt back on, it didn't show at all. No one bothered to watch when he stepped inside different households to visit for a while. Who would ever guess that he was distributing foreign cash to Armenian safe houses?

Just then, Zeki felt the tickle of Jujij's wings against his cheek. He held his breath until the dove hopped down from his shoulder onto his wrist. He opened his hand so she could see the crumbs. He squirmed with delight when Jujij delicately pinched his palm as she ate every morsel of the dried bread. It reminded him of the Armenians. Each crumb of bread they savored like a delicacy. Jujij hopped down from his hand and sat on the edge of the water dish. Zeki marveled at the way she used her beak like a straw to drink up the water. After a few sips, she ruffled her feathers and flew away. Zeki knew she would be back the next day, and so would he.

Zeki stood up and stretched his legs. It was almost time for afternoon prayer. Soon after that it would be time to eat, and he would take plates of food down to the ones hidden in the basement.

He scrambled down the side of the building and was about to step inside when he saw someone leaning against a wall on the other side of the road, reading a newspaper. It was the missionary, John Coren.

Zeki stepped inside the front door of his house, which was also the waiting room for his father's surgery. John Coren crossed the street and followed him in. There was no one else in the waiting room, so Zeki said, "What is it that you want?"

"I need you to follow Khedive the shoemaker tomorrow," said John. "I have to find out if he's trustworthy." John shoved a piece of paper with an address into Zeki's hand and left.

Ten

KEVORK

"You strike a hard bargain, Khedive," said Ahab, Kevork's most successful competitor in the bazaar. Kevork smiled at the hollow compliment as he pocketed four Turkish pounds and handed over the walking boots that Davis no longer needed. Kevork's rucksack felt lighter, but he still had much that weighed on him. As he turned and walked away, Kevork wondered if the money that had been carefully taped to his chest and back was sufficiently hidden under his flowing robe. It didn't rustle, but Kevork knew he was walking more stiffly than usual.

He stepped out of the bazaar and walked past the Citadel. He kept on walking until he reached a small office building surrounded by a high stone wall. Kevork pushed at the wooden door and it opened with ease. Inside was a locked gate. He pulled the bell attached to a rope and waited. It took a few minutes for someone to respond.

"What is your business?" called a man's voice through the door.

"I am here to repair sandals."

The thick door opened just a crack and a single raisin-colored eye appeared. "We cannot afford a shoemaker," said a gruff voice.

"You can pay me with flowers," said Kevork. At the code phrase, the man blinked. Kevork heard the sound of the door unlatch, and then it was pulled open.

52

A man with steel gray hair and a lined face looked Kevork up and down. "I am Reverend MacLaren," said the man. "Come in, come in."

Kevork followed the rector in and waited while the man locked the door. They were standing in a small courtyard that was nothing more than dry dirt. There wasn't a single tree or plant in what must have been a garden at one time. Leaning up against the stone of the walled enclosure were half a dozen children. They were bone-thin and dressed in rags, but they were clean. Their heads were shaved to keep away the lice and their wounds were bandaged. They stared at Kevork with anxious eyes.

"This way," said the rector, gesturing with his hand.

They stepped through the small courtyard to the door of a dusty stone office building. When Reverend MacLaren pushed the door open, the pungent smell of bleaching powder hit Kevork's face like a slap. The rector saw Kevork's change of expression.

"We are battling an outbreak of typhus," said Reverend MacLaren. "The children outside are all healthy, but the ones out back are being treated."

The rector led Kevork into a small room that held a writing desk cluttered with papers and books. He shut the door. "It is safe for you to give me the money here," he said.

"I'll need your help," said Kevork as he slipped off his robe.

The rector opened a desk drawer and took out a pair of scissors. He gingerly snipped at the binding around Kevork's chest. All at once bundles of Turkish pounds slid out.

Kevork pulled his clothing back on and reached into his rucksack. "I have some more money for you here," he said, handing him the cash that he received when he sold the boots he'd made for Leslie Davis.

When Kevork walked back out of the safe house gate, he looked left and right. Nothing appeared suspicious.

He didn't even notice the young Turkish boy leaning up against the wall, feeding pigeons.

⚓

As Kevork walked away from the safe house, he was almost giddy with exhilaration. He had felt powerless and trapped for so long in his guise of Khedive the shoemaker that it thrilled him to be of use finally.

John had warned him not to go back to the Baron Hotel. It was important that the two of them not be linked. "When you're needed again," John had said, "I will find you."

There was no point in opening up his booth at the market this late in the morning. To ensure he wasn't being followed, Kevork wandered through the streets of Aleppo until afternoon prayer. Then he went home.

⚓

When Angele came up to share their usual cup of tea that evening, she saw something different in his expression.

"Did the soldier come back?" she asked.

"It's not that," he said. But he wouldn't tell her what it was.

Angele's eyes went round with panic. "You're not leaving, are you?"

"No," said Kevork. "There is nowhere for me to go." He told her about Leslie Davis not being in Aleppo anymore. Then he told her about the missionary, John Coren. But he didn't tell her about what he had done that morning. The less she knew of his work, the safer it was for them all.

Angele leaned her head against Kevork's shoulder. "I know

you are sad that you cannot get back to Marash, but at least now we can stay together."

Kevork sighed and said, "Even if I had left for Marash, little sister, you know I would have protected you."

Angele looked up at the profile of his face. "Yes, I know that."

～†～

Kevork settled back into his routine at the market. Each day blended into the next as he fixed broken sandal straps, sewed back buckles onto belts, and cut new harnesses for donkeys.

One day, a Turkish boy came to his stall. The boy, who looked vaguely familiar, was so short that he had to stand on his toes to see over the counter of the stall.

"Can you fix these boots?" asked the boy. He opened a bag and drew out a pair of well-worn brown leather boots that looked like they might belong to the boy's father.

Kevork took one of the boots and began to turn it over, but the boy held it to the counter.

"It's the tongue," he said. "I think it is coming loose."

Kevork reached inside the boot and was startled to feel a wad of money. At once he realized where he had seen this boy; he'd been the one feeding pigeons outside the safe house. He locked eyes with the child and said, "It will cost quite a bit to fix these."

"I will pay you in flowers," said the boy under his breath.

Kevork made an effort to keep his face expressionless. "They will be ready tomorrow. Where would you like me to deliver them?"

"Here's the address," said the boy, handing him a folded piece of paper.

After the boy left, Kevork put the boots in his rucksack and continued his work at the stall. When he got home that afternoon, he took the boots out of his sack and drew out the wad of bills. It was even more money than he had delivered the time before. He could leave some of the money shoved deep inside the boots. After all, his ploy would be that he was delivering a repaired set of boots. But what if someone stole the boots? Or, for that matter, simply looked inside? That would be a disaster. Better to tape the money to his body again.

He shoved the money back into the boot for safekeeping as he pondered his dilemma. How could he tape the money to his own chest and back? When he had delivered the money the first time, John Coren had secured the money to his back and wound around lengths of cloth to hold it all in place. Kevork had slept that night with the money on his body, and he woke up at the smallest sound, sure that he had been found out. It had all worked out beautifully in the end, though.

Who could help him wear the money now?

He was still pondering the situation as the sun set and the sky darkened. Angele came up for her after-dinner cup of tea. Of course, thought Kevork to himself. Angele will help me.

"Can I trust you?" he asked her.

Without hesitation she answered, "Yes."

"I need you to help me hide this," he said in a quiet voice, picking up the boot and holding open the flap so she could see the wad of money stuffed inside.

Angele's eyes widened with alarm. It was probably more money than she had ever seen in her life. "Did you steal that?" she whispered.

"No," said Kevork indignantly. Then he told her about his trip to the safe house and about the young boy who delivered the boots that morning.

"That must be Zeki," said Angele matter-of-factly.

"You know this boy?" asked Kevork, surprised.

"He came here the other day asking questions about you," she said with a smile. "But don't worry, we told him only good things."

"Why would you tell a stranger about me?" asked Kevork.

"Zeki Aygun is not a stranger," said Angele. "I know him as well as I know you."

Kevork looked at her in confusion.

"Before I came here, Zeki's mother hid me in her basement."

"Oh!" said Kevork. This was a whole side of Angele that he had not known about.

"How do you want to hide this money?" asked Angele.

Kevork told her of how John Coren had wrapped it onto his body.

"I can do better than that," said Angele with little-girl eagerness.

She hurried down the steps. A moment later she came back, holding an old flour sack similar to the one that she always wore but even more threadbare.

"This is my spare," she said. "Lend me your needle and your leather knife."

Kevork passed the tools over to her and watched her silhouette in the candlelight as she transformed the flour sack into a long sleeve that was big enough to loop over one of his shoulders and around his waist. She fastened long strips of cloth on either end so it could be tied flat and securely. Best of all, it could be reused.

Kevork spread the money out on the rooftop and handed small stacks at a time to Angele, whose delicate fingers deftly placed them into the tube so that they lay flat and side by side. It held all of the bills easily. Then Angele tied each end so the bills wouldn't fall out.

"Let's see how it works," she said. Kevork slipped down his gambaz, holding it tightly with one hand around his waist.

Angele looped the money belt over his shoulder and around his waist, securing it snugly with the long strips of cloth. Kevork pulled the robe back on and tied it.

"Turn around," said Angele.

Kevork turned to the left, then to the right.

"Good," said Angele. "No one will ever know."

Eleven

MARTA

Marta fell asleep with her hands clasped on top of her abdomen. She dreamed that her mother, Parantzim, stood at her bedside—with her hands clasped over her abdomen too. But Parantzim's hands were covered in blood and her abdomen was punctured with bayonet wounds. "I love you, my daughter," said Parantzim. The dream was so real that Marta could feel her mother's presence at her bedside. She could even hear her breathing. Marta opened one eye.

Sarah Baji was standing over her, holding a steaming cup. Marta propped herself up on one elbow and rubbed the sleep out of her eyes.

Sarah perched on the edge of the bed beside Marta's. "I have made you the herbs," she said. "If you want them."

Marta swung her legs over the side of the bed and sat up. She was so close to Sarah Baji that their knees touched. Sarah passed her the cup. Marta took it and sniffed the pungent earthy steam wafting from the cup. She set it down on her lap, her fingers warming to the heat of the brew.

"I don't know if I should drink this," said Marta.

"I will leave you to decide," said Sarah Baji, rising. Her hand brushed gently across Marta's shoulder as she walked toward the door.

Marta brought the cup to her lips. The smell of the steam made her feel slightly nauseous. She looked down into the cup at the swirling bits of leaves and seeds and was again reminded of her mother. Parantzim used to predict the future by reading coffee grounds. She had read Mariam's future but had died before she could read Marta's.

"What future do you see for me, *Mairig* (Mother)?" she asked the cup.

Marta took a sip but didn't swallow. Almost at the same second, she felt a quickening in her abdomen. It was as if the baby knew what she was doing. It startled Marta enough that the cup slipped out of her hands and tumbled to the floor. Marta spat out the liquid that sat on her tongue. "Was that your answer, Mairig?" she said aloud. Then she doubled over in despair, clutching her abdomen.

"What am I going to do now?"

First she wiped the mess up from the floor. Then Marta scrubbed her skin raw with the cold water in the basin. She regarded the Turkish housedress that lay neatly at the end of her bed. It was all the clothing she had brought with her, save the chador, and it was grimy from her recent journey.

She opened the wooden chest that stood beside the basin stand and drew out a plain white cotton blouse that had stiffened with age. She shook it out and draped it over her forearm. Then she pulled out a long dark skirt with an adjustable waistband, and a roomy set of undergarments. The clothing smelled just as musty as the cotton sheets, but putting them on provided her with a sense of security. It was as if she were shedding one skin and donning another. She carefully braided her hair down her back and then looped it tight into a knot so it stayed out of the way.

When she was finished dressing, she looked at herself in the window's reflection. She no longer looked like a Turkish housewife. But what *did* she look like? Not a schoolgirl. In the more constricting clothes, her pregnancy was obvious.

"First things first," said Marta to herself as she stepped out of the dormitory. She still had no idea what to do about the baby in her belly. She did know, however, that she was light-headed with hunger. When was the last time she had eaten? When she lived at the orphanage, they had taken their meals in the huge dining hall. But with so few children here, she had no idea where the meals were currently served. Surely they could all fit in the kitchen. Nevertheless, she walked past the familiar buildings until she got to the dining hall. She could hear childish murmurs from within. She pushed the door open and was met with sudden silence. A dozen pair of eyes looked up at her. At the head of the table sat Miss Younger and beside her was Sarah Baji. There were no other adults. A bowl of dried figs, currants, and apricots sat in the middle of the table, and there was a platter of flat bread and an urn filled with tea.

The girls, who looked as young as six and as old as perhaps ten or eleven, sat along each side of the long table, faces freshly washed and hair combed and neatly braided down each back. At the end of one side sat the two boys, who both looked younger than the youngest girl. They too were neatly groomed and healthy looking. It was odd to see boys in the Bethel dining hall when Beitshalom was on the other side of the complex. With a pang, Marta realized they were the only rescued boys. It made Marta wonder about how they got here. After all, the streets were filled with urchins. If children could just walk in, wouldn't all those orphans be here? She would have to ask Miss Younger about how these fortunate children happened to be here.

"Come. Sit," said Miss Younger, patting the back of an empty chair across from Sarah Baji.

Marta walked in, acutely conscious of the eyes staring at her belly with open curiosity. She pulled out the chair and sat down.

Miss Younger tapped her knuckle on the table. "Children," she said, "this is Marta Hovsepian. She has come to help us."

The children whispered excitedly to one another, grinning and pointing at Marta. Miss Younger tapped her knuckle again. "Let us continue with our breakfast," she said.

The children went back to their flat bread and fruit, stealing furtive glances at Marta when they thought Miss Younger wasn't looking.

Marta poured herself some tea. She put a handful of dried fruit on her plate and reached for a piece of bread. The food was simple, but it smelled delicious. It surprised her that she could be even remotely interested in food, given the momentous choices she had to make about her life, her future.

As she pulled off a bit of bread and set it on her tongue, she looked up and met Sarah Baji's eyes. She shook her head. Sarah Baji nodded in understanding. Miss Younger's shoulders relaxed visibly.

"Stay and help us for as long as you can," said Miss Younger. "And when your time comes, we will help you."

Marta looked first at Miss Younger and then at Sarah Baji. The love and caring that she saw in their eyes brought tears to her own.

"Thank you," she said.

>[†]

Marta settled in to the daily routine at the orphanage. Miss Younger didn't want her to do any strenuous work. And with so few children, there wasn't that much to be done. She taught the children their lessons each morning, and she assisted Sarah Baji in the kitchen in the afternoons.

Once a week, Miss Younger tackled the laundry. It was an

arduous task. Even though she insisted this would be too strenuous for someone with child, Marta would help her sort the clothing and scrub out the stains with a bar of soap and a scrub board. The laundry tub was huge. After all, it was the one that had been used for the whole orphanage. To make money for the orphanage, Miss Younger took in laundry for a few of the wealthier Turkish families. Between that and a week's worth of dirty clothing from a dozen children, the laundry tub would be filled to the brim each week.

Miss Younger filled the tub with bucket after bucket of water. Once Marta had scrubbed the worst stains out, she and Miss Younger would put all the light-colored clothing into the vat and heat it until it was boiling. The process was repeated for the dark clothing. While Miss Younger poked and stirred the laundry with a long stick, Marta would keep her company. Sometimes they would talk about the various children and the antics they had been up to. Other times they speculated about when the war would be over.

One day Marta broached a more sensitive topic. "Why can't the street urchins be brought in here?" she asked.

Miss Younger brushed a strand of gray-blonde hair out of her eyes with the back of her hand and sighed. "When you arrived, did you not notice the soldiers at the gate?"

"I saw them," said Marta.

"They keep the children away," replied Miss Younger.

"But why?" asked Marta. "You would think they'd be happy to get the children off the street."

"You don't understand," said Miss Younger. "The urchins are not supposed to exist. They were already deported once, but some of them found their way back to Marash. Each day wagons go up and down the streets, looking for urchins. The soldiers pick them up and take them away."

"To where?" asked Marta.

"I can only speculate," replied Miss Younger. "But I think they are deported into the desert once again."

"How did you rescue the few who are here?" asked Marta.

"These few are the lucky ones," said Miss Younger. "We managed to smuggle them in, hidden in supply carts. Some were rescued by Turks and brought to us."

"How is it that they are safe here?" asked Marta.

"Diplomacy," said Miss Younger. "This is a German mission, and the Germans are allied with the Turks in this war. So they turn a blind eye as long as we do not provide refuge for Armenians over the age of thirteen. They don't take note of old women either, which is why they haven't come to get Sarah Baji."

"Is my presence putting everyone in danger?" asked Marta.

Miss Younger leaned heavily on her laundry paddle and sighed. After a moment she straightened her shoulders and looked Marta in the eye. "It is a risk we are willing to take," she said.

Marta gulped back tears. She was so grateful to have refuge at the orphanage, but it frightened her to think of the risk she had placed on them. And the worst of it was that it was beyond her control. Where could she possibly go? She would have to think hard about a good place to hide if the orphanage was ever raided.

Miss Younger said nothing for quite some time. She stirred the steamy brew of dirty clothing and cast furtive glances at Marta. She looked as if there were something she wanted to say but didn't know how.

"Have you found something out about Kevork?" Marta blurted.

"No," said Miss Younger. "Not about Kevork."

"But about someone?" asked Marta. What was it that Miss Younger was keeping from her?

Miss Younger concentrated on her stirring as if her life

depended on it. She glanced up once and opened her mouth as if to say something but stopped again.

"You will have to tell me at some point," said Marta. "Please tell me now. I have a right to know."

Miss Younger pulled the laundry paddle out of the tub and balanced it across the top. She sat beside Marta and cradled her hands in her own. The older woman looked intently into Marta's eyes.

"Your sister is alive," she said.

Marta gasped. "But that is good news, isn't it?"

"Perhaps," said Miss Younger. "But I don't know if you will see it that way."

"What do you mean?" asked Marta.

"She has married Rustem Bey and adopted the Muslim faith."

Marta regarded Miss Younger in confusion. "That cannot be right," she said. "Rustem Bey proposed to her, but she said no."

Miss Younger sighed. "I can only tell you what I saw with my eyes," she replied. "Mariam came here with Rustem nearly a year ago. She was dressed in Turkish attire, right down to the henna on her hands."

"But she could have been dressed like that to avoid deportation," said Marta.

"Why would she tell *me* that she was Rustem's wife?" asked Miss Younger. "In fact, they adopted a child from the orphanage."

Marta's head was spinning with the news. She was relieved that Mariam was alive. After all, the last time she had seen her sister was when she was carried off by the Turkish captain. Marta hadn't been able to face what might have happened after that. How had Mariam ended up in Rustem Bey's home? It hardly mattered. The important thing was that she was alive.

"What child did they adopt?" asked Marta.

"They took little Parantzim," said Miss Younger. "Do you remember her? She came to the orphanage the day before the deportations."

Marta nodded in recognition. "Rustem and Mariam saved Parantzim from deportation."

"Yes," said Miss Younger.

Twelve

KEVORK

Kevork rose the next morning at the first call to prayer, just before sunrise. In the darkness, he gathered his rucksack, placing inside it the boots that Zeki had brought him. He unfolded the piece of paper with the address written on it, memorized it, and stuffed it back into the folds of his clothing. He walked down the earthen steps and passed the girls, all asleep by their looms.

As he passed Angele, she sat up in the darkness. "Be safe," she whispered.

"I'll try," he answered.

There weren't many people on the narrow cobbled streets at this time of the morning. Kevork made fast progress to his destination to the edge of town. It was an old wooden house with ornately carved shutters. He admired the richness of the patterned wood and marveled at the fact that there was no telltale smell of disease or bleaching powder. The street was almost empty. He pulled the rope on the bell at the gate and waited.

Five minutes passed and no one answered. The sun was rising, and activity was increasing on the street. He pulled the rope again, shifting from one foot to the other. He hoped he had the right place.

Several minutes passed, then the gate opened a few inches. Kevork could see the blue eye and pale skin of a woman with unnaturally red hair. "I have repaired your boots," he said.

67

"I have no money to pay you," said the woman.

"You can pay me in flowers," whispered Kevork, looking from left to right. A man had just passed by. Kevork prayed that he hadn't heard.

The door opened wide and Kevork felt a hand on his forearm, pulling him in. The woman swiftly fastened the door behind him. "This way," she said, walking briskly through the dusty inner courtyard and up a set of creaking wooden steps to dark wooden double doors that were burnished with age.

It was a huge house, a mansion as far as Kevork could tell. So when he followed the woman through the double doors, he expected the luxury of the Baron Hotel. Instead, what he saw was more institutional. There were no carpets on the floor or walls and all of the surfaces had been scrubbed clean and coated with an acrid-smelling layer of lime. All of the rooms in the front of the house were empty, but Kevork could hear the sound of childish whispers coming from somewhere at the back of the house. The words he could make out were Armenian.

The redheaded woman led him into a small room that held nothing but a battered wooden table, one chair, and an oriental sofa piled high with clean cotton tunics and shirts. The table was littered with papers and ledgers. A telegraph machine attached to wires was positioned at the edge of the table.

Kevork had seen a telegraph machine once before when he had delivered repaired boots to the police station. It startled him to see the machine here, with this woman.

"You're a German missionary?" asked Kevork in Arabic, extending his hand.

The woman nodded. "My name is Amelia Schultz."

"This is a legal orphanage, not a safe house?" asked Kevork.

"For the present, yes," replied the woman. "It is only a matter of time before all the German orphanages are closed down for good."

Kevork heard the news with dismay. "But the Germans and Turks are allies in the war," he said. "Why would they shut down the German orphanages?"

"We are an embarrassment to them all," replied Miss Schultz wearily. "There aren't supposed to be any orphans to save."

Kevork sighed with frustration. The German missions had been in Turkey for decades. In his own lifetime, he had witnessed two Armenian massacres, the Adana Massacre of 1909 and the deportations in 1915. His father had been a survivor of the 1896 massacres. How many generations of Armenians would have been lost if it hadn't been for people like this Miss Schultz and Miss Younger, his own orphanage supervisor?

Kevork looked from Miss Schultz to the telegraph machine on her desk. An outrageous thought came to him. He asked in German, "Do you know Josefine Younger from the Bethel and Beitshalom Orphanages in Marash?"

The woman's eyes widened in surprise. "You speak German well," she said warily.

"I was taught at Beitshalom," replied Kevork.

"I see," said Miss Schultz, nodding in recognition. "I know Miss Younger. In fact," she said, gesturing toward the telegraph machine, "we communicate on a regular basis."

Kevork could feel his heart thumping in his throat. If she could communicate with the orphanage, then what was stopping her from finding out right now if Marta was there?

"Can you send Miss Younger a message from me?" asked Kevork.

"I can," sighed Miss Schultz wearily. "Here is a pen and paper," she said, pulling a blank sheet from the mess on her table and handing him a fountain pen. "Write it out for me and I shall send it as soon as I have the time. Please keep it brief. I am going to check on the children. I shall be back in a few moments."

Kevork sat down on the wooden chair and gently moved some of the papers on the desk to make a space for his own. As much as he longed to know the truth about Marta, now that the moment had come to find out, he was afraid. What if she was dead? What would be the point of living then? But he swallowed his fear and wrote,

> To Josefine Younger from Kevork Adomian. Do you have any information about Marta Hovsepian? Please respond care of Amelia Schultz.

Kevork set the pen down on the table and then leaned back in the chair. It was a simple message, but those twenty words held his life in the balance.

The moments ticked by and Miss Schultz did not come back. As he waited, Kevork gazed about the room. It looked like it had been set up in a hurry. It was no more personal than the lime-washed rooms at the front of the house. His eyes were drawn to the papers scattered across the desk. He didn't want to read them—they were private, after all—but the word *Armenians* on a telegram written in Turkish jumped out at him. He leaned forward and read:

> From: Ministry of the Interior
> Date: June 27, 1916
> To: Amelia Schultz, German Missionary, Aleppo
> The Turkish government is pleased to announce that
> Armenian children over the age of thirteen currently in the
> care of foreign missions will be relocated to the camp at Deir

*Ez Zor for their safety. Armenian adults under the employ of
foreign missions will accompany the children. Compliance to
this measure is to be completed within forty-eight hours.
Refusal to do so will result in the closure of your mission.*

Deir Ez Zor? thought Kevork in horror. That was in the heart
of the Syrian Desert. This was no "relocation." It was deportation
and death. In fact, it was the same place that Kevork himself had
been taken to the year before. He had been forced to dig his own
grave, then was shot and left for dead. Had it not been for Huda
and her Arab clan, his bones would now be turning to dust in the
desert. It also made him realize how unlikely it was that Marta
would be at the orphanage in Marash. Wouldn't Miss Younger
have the same "relocation" order to contend with?

Kevork looked up and saw Miss Schultz standing in the doorway, her sleeves rolled up and her arms still damp to the elbow. By
the stricken look on her face, it was clear that she knew he had
read the telegram.

"That is just one of my current problems," she said wearily. "I
need to keep the little ones here clean and fed. And I have been trying to get food to the ones already in the relocation camps, but the
authorities have blocked any more missionaries from traveling there."

Kevork knew from his own experience that because of the vast
numbers of deportees, the government preferred to kill them by
starvation and exposure rather than with bullets. Nomadic families who lived in the desert were happy to sell food and water to
the deportees, but they charged exorbitant fees.

Kevork stood up and pointed to the money belt under his
clothing. "There is plenty of money here," he said.

Miss Schultz sighed. "Money is of no use if we can't get it into
the camps."

71

A moment passed. Then two. Miss Schultz regarded Kevork steadily. There was a look of challenge in her eyes.

Finally, Kevork said, "Do you want me to go?"

It was a huge risk to go into the concentration camps and distribute the money, and Kevork knew it. The deportees were watched over by Turkish soldiers and mercenaries who didn't tolerate interference. But he couldn't live with himself if he didn't try.

Amelia Schultz helped him untie the money belt, and then she sorted the pile into small bundles. "You've got to be able to grab a bundle of money at a moment's notice when the soldiers aren't looking," she explained. "Hand it to missionaries or priests if you see any, otherwise, use your judgment and hand them to whomever seems to be helping and managing."

On top of his own gambaz, Miss Schultz gave him several other robes to wear. These were also to distribute. He emptied his rucksack of all his tools, leaving only his small prayer rug inside.

"I'll keep these safe until you come back," Miss Schultz said, wrapping his tools into a cloth and setting them in the corner of the room.

Then she helped him fill his rucksack with individual cloth packets of nuts and raisins.

"This won't get you very far," said Miss Schultz. "But the camps begin almost as soon as you leave the city."

"I will do my best," he said. And then he left.

⤛⸙⤜

Miss Schultz watched him out of the window as he walked down the street. Then she returned to her desk. His message to Miss Younger lay on top of the other papers. In her heart, she knew that the right thing to do was to send this telegraph. But John Coren had warned her that Kevork might ask this of her. He told her that under no circumstances should she send the message on. He explained that they needed Kevork's talent as a courier. What would happen to the thousands of starving Armenians if Kevork ran off to find his Marta? Wasn't humanity best served if he thought her dead? Amelia couldn't argue the point, but in her heart she felt John was wrong. She didn't send the telegraph, but she didn't destroy the message either.

Maybe later, she thought. Let's just wait and see.

As Kevork walked out of the southern gates of Aleppo and down the familiar dusty road that led to the Syrian Desert, he wondered whether he would ever return. How terrible it would be if Marta were at the orphanage and she got the telegram that he was alive, only to find out later that he had died. But in times of war, how many loved ones suffered this fate? Kevork knew that he wasn't special. All he could do was follow his conscience and hope for the best. Perhaps it would comfort her to know that he had lived a bit longer.

He could smell the first concentration camp a mile away. The sickly sweet odor of disease and death came to him in waves with the hot desert breeze. Soon he could hear it: crying babies and children, the screaming of mothers, and the groans of people in death throes. One person making these sounds would have been bad enough, but multiplied by the thousands there was no more hellish sound on earth.

When the camp finally came into view, it was a horizon of tattered tents, spanning as far as the eye could see. Kevork walked toward the encampment, dreading what he would find. He took measured breaths, not wanting to take in any more of the fetid air than necessary.

The first tent he reached was pitched by itself on the outskirts of the camp. At first he thought it was abandoned, but then he heard faint singing from inside. He reached out to the ragged flap and pulled it open. A wave of putrid odor slapped him in the face. Holding his breath, Kevork crouched down to look inside. There lay a woman whose wizened face was shriveled like a discarded apple. On her lap was a child swollen in death and loosely wrapped in a lice-encrusted blanket. The woman rocked the child back and forth and cooed lovingly into her ear, seemingly oblivious to the fact that the child was dead. She didn't seem to notice the lice in the blanket or the maggots in the child's open wounds.

"Mairig," said Kevork gently. "Let me help you bury the child."

The woman looked up, startled. She frowned for a moment, then she looked back down at the child in her arms. She sighed deeply and said, "Yes, it is time for Keran to meet her maker."

Kevork delicately dismantled the tent, trying his best not to disturb the woman. As he did so, hundreds of lice fled the dirty blanket and burrowed into the sand. Kevork found a rock and scraped out a shallow grave in the sand. He took the child's body from the woman and gently laid it down. As he helped the woman to her feet, the cloth that covered her hair slipped off and he realized that she wasn't as old as he thought she was. Although her face was wizened with starvation and grief, her braided hair was jet black and as thick as a man's fist. Perhaps she was only a decade older than Kevork. She walked to where her child lay in the shallow grave, scooped up a handful of sand, and sprinkled it over the corpse, saying the traditional prayer as she did so. Then Kevork and the woman buried the child, a handful of sand at a time.

Kevork pressed a packet of raisins into her hand. He left her standing vigil over the grave of her daughter. He continued on his way toward the camp. He passed a cluster of soldiers, leaning on their bayonets and smoking cigarettes. One looked at him disinterestedly as he walked by.

Each tent that Kevork encountered was a scene of family tragedy. He didn't think his heart could ache any more than it already did, but he was wrong. Tents were pitched and the sick and dying lay inside, without food or water to ease their pain. Those who were not yet too sick limped up to Kevork and tugged at his robes. "Food, food, water, food!" they cried. After a while, he panicked and began to hit away their hands. It was all too overwhelming.

One of the Turkish soldiers slung his bayonet over his shoulder and approached Kevork. "What is your business?" he asked in Arabic.

"Home," said Kevork, pointing southeast, along the deportation route.

The soldier regarded Kevork intently. Kevork could feel his gaze on his Arabic headdress and robe, and his distinctive blue tattoos.

"Go," said the soldier. "But don't bother these people," and he gestured toward the pitiful cluster of people who were extending their arms toward Kevork, as if to merely touch him would somehow provide them with food.

Kevork nodded to the soldier and continued on his way. He could feel the soldier's eyes on his back, so he made a swatting motion with his hands at the deportees. "Get away, you filth," he hissed.

He walked through the center of the concentration camp, looking straight ahead like a horse with blinders. All the while, his heart was full of sorrow. How he wished he could help these people. There were thousands, and every one of them was in dire circumstances. Here he was, money and food hidden in packets all over his body. But how could he help?

He walked past a wagon that was stacked with the still-breathing bodies of women and children. He tried not to react as soldiers unloaded them as if they were logs of wood. One of the women cried in agony as she hit the ground; Kevork's stomach churned. A soldier threw a dead child on top of the woman, and she cried again.

Kevork walked on.

Ahead of him, a crowd of deportees clustered around a fountain. A Kurd was sitting on a wooden stool with a ladle in his hand. As each deportee approached the Kurd, he ladled them a single cup of water in exchange for a coin, a wedding ring, or an earring.

Kevork looked around. No soldiers in sight.

A young woman sat on the ground at the edge of the crowd. She was not much older than Marta had been when Kevork had last seen her. The woman's feet were bare and covered with blisters and all she had on was a tattered cotton shift that didn't even cover her knees. Her eyes were round with hunger and her cheeks were hollow, but she did not grasp at Kevork as he passed by. She was caressing the fevered brow of a young boy who was asleep in her lap. The boy was as thin as she was, but his feet were not blistered. Had she carried him all this way?

He crouched down until he was eye level with her. She looked up at him momentarily, then looked back down at the child in her lap. That brief glimpse was like looking into her soul. Kevork gasped and held back a sob. So many Armenians sitting in the desert, waiting to die.

"Can you do something for me?" Kevork asked her gently.

She looked back up at him again, and the cold acceptance in her eyes chilled him to the bone. What all had she done for men to stay alive?

"Not that," he said.

She looked confused. He reached into the folds of his robe and drew out a stack of bills. "Wait until I am out of sight," he said. "Then pay that man to give water to these people here."

The woman looked down at the stack of money and her eyes widened. She looked up at him and almost smiled. "God is with you," she said.

Kevork drew out a small packet of nuts and one of raisins. "These are for you and the child," he said, dropping the packets into the sand by her side. He stood up and walked briskly away.

As he continued to walk through the camp, the intensity of the suffering around him was overwhelming.

He passed an elderly man who was stripping clothing off corpses and laying the clothing out in the sun to bake away the lice. Kevork walked up to him, "What are you doing with that clothing?" he asked, trying to make sure that his voice sounded non-confrontational.

Kevork expected the man to cower and flee, but instead, he held himself up straight and looked Kevork in the eye. "I am distributing them to those who still live," said the man.

"How much are you charging?" asked Kevork.

The man's eyes narrowed in disgust. "I am not about to make a profit on the sufferings of my fellow countrymen and women," he said. "They take them when they're ready." He pointed to a cluster of women in the distance who were picking clothing up off the ground.

Kevork nodded in approval. Then he said, "Is there any place to buy food here?"

"For cash," replied the old man bitterly. "But who has that?"

"Where do you get food for cash?" asked Kevork.

"A group of enterprising Arabs comes each morning with fresh water and bread to sell, but it's very expensive."

Kevork looked around. There were no soldiers in the immediate area. He slipped off his top robe, then reached into the depths of his inner robe and pulled out a bundle of cash and some nuts and raisins. He wrapped the robe around the cash and food and handed it to the man.

The old man watched Kevork at first with confusion, then with joy. "Bless you," he said, taking the bundle.

Kevork turned and continued on his way. The help he had brought here was just a drop of rain in the desert. Even if he managed to distribute all of the pitiful packets of nuts and dried fruit and the meager bits of money, could he actually save any of these people? By sheer force of will, he pushed those thoughts away. If he could save even one, his mission would be a success.

He passed a cluster of Turkish soldiers sitting on camp stools, playing cards and smoking cigarettes. "Hey you!" called one. "Come join us."

Kevork looked around. They could only be talking to him. He walked over uncertainly and stood before them. "Sit," said an older soldier with a glistening black mustache. He pointed to an empty camp stool across from him.

Kevork took a deep calming breath, then sat down, turning his knees to face the soldier who had invited him to sit.

"What are you doing amidst all these infidels?" asked the soldier, lighting a second cigarette from the tip of the one dangling from his mouth. "Don't you know you can get a disease from being here?"

The other soldiers laughed at this comment.

"I'm going home," said Kevork, pointing farther southeast into the desert. "This is the direct route."

"Here," said the soldier, passing the lit cigarette to Kevork. "This will help get the stink of the *giaours* (infidels) out of your nostrils."

Kevork took the cigarette and put it to his lips. He had to admit that the smell of cigarette smoke was a welcome relief from the odor of death. "Thank you," said Kevork.

"If you go that way," said the soldier, pointing directly south. "You'll have a quieter journey."

Kevork nodded. "Thanks," he said. "I shall take your advice."

"Let me walk you part of the way," said the soldier, standing up.

Kevork stood up too, keeping the cigarette in his mouth and trying to stay calm. Had the soldier guessed what he was up to? What would he do to him?

They walked in silence side by side for fifteen minutes or more. The pitiful deportees who were in their pathway cringed in terror. Finally, when they were close to the edge of the encampment, the soldier said, "I saw you give that bundle to the old man."

Kevork's heart was in his mouth. He didn't know what to say. Perhaps he should run? But the soldier had a gun. He could simply shoot him, then loot his body.

"You're working for the missionaries, aren't you?" said the soldier.

"Yes," Kevork admitted, staring defiantly into the soldier's eyes.

The soldier held his gaze for a moment. Then he said, "Good luck with that."

Kevork's jaw dropped.

"These massacres will be the ruin of Turkey," said the soldier. "I am no happier about this than you are."

"But...but...you're assisting them," sputtered Kevork, more in shock than rage.

"I have not killed a single Armenian," answered the soldier, "And I help where I can. But we are at war. I obey my orders."

The two men stood staring at each other for another long moment.

"You are not a bad man," said Kevork.

The soldier laughed bitterly. "Nor are you."

"Perhaps you will help me?" asked Kevork. Even as the words tumbled out of his mouth, he was in awe at his own audacity. Or was it stupidity?

"Here is some money," said Kevork. He reached into the folds of his robe and pulled out a bundle of cash. "Can you get food for some of those people?"

The soldier's eyes filled with tears. "Yes," he said. "I will try. And if I get killed while trying, then it is Allah's will."

The soldier stuffed the bills inside his uniform jacket, then walked back to the camp. Kevork watched him go, then turned southeast, toward the next concentration camp.

Thirteen

MISS YOUNGER

Josefine Younger closed the door after stepping into her office and then sat down at her desk. She thought about Marta's arrival six months earlier. It had stirred up a host of memories for her. Memories and problems. It was so good to see Marta alive. More than that, she seemed to be emotionally unscathed, which was a miracle in itself. Miss Younger could only imagine the horrors she had lived through. And this pregnancy! There was no nurse or doctor on staff, and Marta was almost due. Thank goodness for Sarah Baji. Sarah had delivered more than one baby. Marta would be in good hands.

But the real problem was that if the Turks found out that Marta was hiding at the orphanage, they would come in and get her. She would be deported yet again. Miss Younger shuddered to think of Marta, big with child, forced at the point of a bayonet and taken to some godforsaken place in the desert. How could she ensure that Marta was never found? She bowed her head and rested it on her forearms.

"Please, God," she said, "tell me what to do." She closed her eyes and almost fell asleep, but a tick-ticking roused her. A telegraph was arriving.

She stared at the telegraph machine as it spit out its message. When it stopped ticking, Miss Younger tore off the paper and held it in front of her. It read:

> *From: German Embassy, Constantinople*
> *Date: July 22, 1916*
> *To: Josefine Younger, German Missionary, Marash*
> *It has come to our attention that you are harboring illegal*
> *Armenians at your orphanage. You are becoming an embarrass-*
> *ment to our government. You are ordered to return to Germany.*
> *A car will come for you on July 23, 1916, at noon. Please be ready.*

No! This could not be happening! How could she save Marta and her baby now? Miss Younger rested her head back down on her forearms and wept.

⚜

The next day Miss Younger stood inside the gates of the orphanage. At her feet was a single worn leather satchel, hastily packed. Her eyes were swollen from crying, and her hair had been wound into a careless bun. All the children were lined up, silent in their sadness, eyes round with grief. Miss Younger walked up to each child and said her good-bye. At the end of the line stood Sarah Baji, and then Marta.

"I know that you can manage without me," said Miss Younger as she hugged Sarah Baji. The tremor in her voice belied her words.

"You have done so much for the children," said Sarah Baji. "And we thank you for that."

Miss Younger then turned to Marta. "Be safe, my dear," she said. "I hate leaving you in this condition."

Marta wrapped her arms around Miss Younger and breathed in her familiar clean scent one last time. It devastated her to lose this woman who had become like a mother to her. She had promised herself that she wouldn't cry, but she couldn't help it. As she hugged Miss Younger good-bye, the tears rolled down her face. "Please be safe," she said. "And please write us if you can."

"I shall," said Miss Younger. She picked up her satchel and then stood up straight, taking in a deep breath and squaring her shoulders. She walked to the car and opened the door. Just before she got in, she turned and waved one last time. The gates opened and the car drove away just as the muezzins began to call the midday prayer.

☜†☞

Marta was utterly bereft without Miss Younger. She was too big with child to be of much use, and Sarah Baji was too old to do all the work herself. The children took on many of the tasks, but between the laundry, the cooking, the cleaning, and the general maintenance, it was just too overwhelming for one old woman and a pregnant young one to accomplish.

So when the orphanage gates opened again a week after Miss Younger had been driven away, Marta peered out the classroom window in anticipation. A shiny black car with its top rolled down entered the yard.

"Class dismissed," said Marta to the children. They all ran out to see who had arrived. Marta opened the window enough so she could hear, and then she watched from the corner of the window.

The driver was a young Turkish officer of some sort. There were two passengers. One was a small woman with intelligent brown eyes and a curly mop of short light brown hair. She didn't look much older than Marta, but she did look like she meant business. She was dressed in a dark blue wool cape even though the weather was quite warm, and she carried a black leather satchel. The other passenger was a bald man with a monocle and a rather large brown suitcase. He too was dressed for the weather of some other country.

Once the car left and the gates closed again, Marta came out from the classroom.

"Hello, hello!" the man greeted her. "My name is Mr. Brighton, and I have come from America."

Marta understood enough English to know that he had just introduced himself, but when she looked around at Sarah Baji and the children, she knew that they were at a complete loss. She stepped forward and held out her hand.

"My name is Marta Hovsepian," she said in halting English, "and this is Sarah Baji." She gestured toward the dozen children who stared at him in curiosity. "And these are all the children we have at the moment."

"We must do something about that," said Mr. Brighton with a crisp smile. "I saw many children in need of help as we drove into the city."

Marta nodded in agreement. Did he have a way of sneaking those poor urchins into the orphanage complex? She would be forever grateful to him if he did.

Mr. Brighton took the elbow of the lady who stood beside him. "This is Miss Bowley," he said. "She is a nurse from America."

Marta grinned with delight. A nurse was the answer to her prayers. She had a suspicion that her baby would be arriving any day now.

"Greetings," said Nurse Bowley in halting Armenian as she stepped out of the car and into the dusty courtyard. "I am happy to make your acquaintance."

Fourteen

KEVORK

As Kevork's journey took him toward the Euphrates River, he encountered a number of small deportee encampments. Some with soldiers, but others on their own, without food or water, and in some instances without any clothing. He looked carefully at each woman's face, almost afraid that he would find Marta. It was somewhere along this route that they had been separated.

By the time he got to his last stop, Meskene, he had become disheartened to the point of numbness.

But when he entered Meskene, he was surprised to find no soldiers. Had they not bothered to come this far? Perhaps they assumed that anyone who had reached this point would die of exposure. But as he walked past clusters of people and pitched tents, he was struck by an unfamiliar smell. He had been so accustomed to breathing in the stench of human corpses that its absence was bewildering. Also absent was the constant roar of groans and screams. The thousands here were thin, but they weren't starving. They were dressed in rags, but the rags were clean and not squirming with lice.

He crouched down to talk to a boy who was giving his young sister a bit of water from a tin cup.

"Who is in charge?" he asked the boy in Armenian.

The boy looked into Kevork's face. He didn't smile, but he

wasn't distressed either. So very strange. "Sister Helena," he replied, pointing toward a tent at the center of the encampment.

Kevork walked over to the tent and lifted the canvas flap. "Is Sister Helena here?" he asked in German.

"Who asks?" a surprisingly youthful voice responded.

Kevork bent down so that he could see inside the tent. Within the dimness, he saw an elderly man, the stillness of near death hovering over him. At his side was an angel. He blinked and realized that it was a young nun dressed in white.

The nun's eyes locked onto Kevork's. "I will be with you in a moment," she said.

Kevork stood up and let the canvas flap fall back down. As he waited for Sister Helena, he marveled at the novelty of what was happening in the tent. An Armenian man dying in dignity and comfort? Kevork brought his hands to his face and his chest heaved with emotion. A small kindness after so much inhumanity was almost too much to bear.

He felt a touch on his shoulder. He raised his head. There stood the angel. The nun. Sister Helena.

"Do you need help?" she asked, her voice filled with compassion.

Kevork breathed in deeply to compose himself. "No," he replied. "I came to help you."

As they walked through the camp together, Sister Helena showed Kevork her makeshift sanitation station. A row of children were lined up obediently. A few of the healthier women deportees were cutting off the children's hair, stripping off their rags, and getting the children to stand in big metal tubs so they could be washed and deloused.

She took him to another part of the camp. There, a group of deportees were washing rags and laying them out in the sun to dry.

Kevork was amazed. "The soldiers don't come here?" he asked.

"They haven't," she said. "Although they may at some point."

"Where are you getting your supplies?" he asked.

"I brought money with me from Germany," she said. "We purchase what we can from the Kurds and Arabs in the desert."

"That's expensive," he said.

"Yes," she replied. "We have made do so far. God provides."

<center>~~~†~~~</center>

That night, he sat on a rock beside her in the firelight and touched the wedding ring on his baby finger.

"Were you married?" Sister Helena asked.

"Betrothed," he said. "The last time I saw her was around here. A year ago."

They shared a pot of weak tea and some hard crackers. As Kevork blew at the steam swirling out of his tin cup, he regarded the nun in the flickering light. A wisp of her light brown hair had escaped from her white veil. In her demeanor and determination, she reminded him of Miss Younger. But where Miss Younger was middle-aged, Sister Helena was not much older than Kevork. He was awed by her dedication and stamina. What was it that had brought her here to the desert to help Armenian deportees, when she could have stayed in her comfortable life in Germany? She caught him looking at her and gave him a tired smile.

"May I stay for a while and help you?" Kevork asked.

"I would like that," she replied.

<center>~~~†~~~</center>

Helena insisted that Kevork be deloused and washed too, although he refused to have his hair cut, pointing out that it was part of his Arab disguise. Then he assisted her by cooking huge vats of sorghum and water into a porridge and serving up the gloppy mess to the never-ending lineup of children, women, and grandparents who had arrived at the concentration camp.

On his third morning at Meskene, Kevork woke up before sunrise with a raging headache. He tried to ignore it and got up as usual, but by the time he had purchased the day's supply of sorghum from a Kurdish family and carried the basket of grain back to the massive cooking pot, he began to have spasms of pain in his legs.

He tried to carry a bucket of water over to the cooking pot, but his legs gave way and he fell over. By this time, the muscle spasms were in his shoulders and chest too and his headache still raged. As he lay in the sand, he gripped his knees to his chest and groaned in agony. Never in his life had he experienced such excruciating physical pain.

Then he felt a cool hand on his forehead. He tried to open his eyes, but the sunlight felt like a knife in his eyes so he kept them squeezed shut. "You've got typhus," Helena's voice stated.

It was an unending nightmare.

Flashbacks of the day he lost Marta tormented him.

He stared at Marta lovingly. After days and weeks of marching through the desert, she still had a look of determination. Where other girls had been raped and killed, her disguise—hair shorn, and wearing a pair of his trousers and a boy's shirt—had protected her. But now they had been ordered into separate groups, and Marta refused to leave his side.

"This is suicide," he whispered to her harshly, pushing her away.

"I will not leave you," she said.

A soldier pulled her roughly back to the other group and in doing so, ripped her shirt, exposing a breast. He grinned.

"Friends, I've got a girl here!"

Just then, Kevork's aunt came from out of nowhere. She grabbed a bayonet from a nearby soldier's hands and lunged at the man who was holding Marta. He saw her coming and ducked in the nick of time. Then the deportees and soldiers watched in horror as Aunt Anna lunged again, missing the soldier completely, but stabbing Captain Mahmoud Sayyid in the neck.

"That is for Mariam," she said fiercely.

Time stood still. Soldiers and deportees alike stared as the man collapsed, blood soaking his uniform. The soldier who was holding on to Marta was as mesmerized by the scene as everyone else.

"Run!" shouted Anna. Marta pulled away from her captor and dashed into the crowd.

"Infidel!" cried the soldier. And with one swift movement, he pierced Anna's heart with his bayonet.

Then he turned to deal with Marta. But she had vanished.

Kevork knew exactly where in the crowd she was hiding, but he didn't look. He willed himself to keep his eyes on his dying aunt. That was the last time he had seen Marta alive.

He felt the wedding ring on his baby finger and twisted it, trying to take it off and give it to the phantom in his memory.

"Dear Marta!" he cried. "I love you! Please come back!"

Then he felt a hand cupping the back of his head while another hand held a tin cup of cool water to his lips.

He remembered convulsions of shivering followed by the torments of heat, and lying in a pool of sweat, looking up at the weave work of the flimsy tent that covered him. But mostly he remembered nothing.

Then one day he opened his eyes. Sister Helena sat beside him on a camp stool, a tin of water in her hands and a look of concern in her eyes. He tried to sit up, but he was too dizzy and fell back again. He held his hands up to his face. They felt so heavy that it was like lifting the huge vat of sorghum. His arms were covered with spots that looked like dull reddish sores that had healed—the classic sign of someone who has survived typhus.

"How long have I been sick?" he asked.

"Three weeks," Sister Helena replied in a tired voice. Then she reached toward him, grabbed his arms, and helped him sit up.

"I haven't helped you much," he said.

"You almost died."

He was too weak to walk back to Aleppo and he was too weak to be of much use to Sister Helena. But he did what he could for her while he regained his strength. The overwhelming workload made Sister Helena wild with despair and frustration.

Kevork understood her personal hell. She could work from morning until night, day after day, but nothing could stop fate. Each morning, a hundred or more deportees would die, and in the afternoon, a hundred or more new deportees would arrive to take their place.

After a month, Kevork was strong enough to leave. Before he did, he gave her all of the money that he had left. Then he turned north and walked back to Aleppo. On the journey back, he avoided all the camps, keeping to the west and away from prying eyes.

Fifteen

MARTA

Marta's hands rested gently on her huge belly as she gazed out of the window of the dormitory. She watched two young boys in their flour-sack tunics kick a sheep's bladder ball back and forth to each other. It was good to see them in a wholesome activity for a change.

Since Mr. Brighton and Nurse Bowley had arrived, there had been an influx of orphans. Marta didn't exactly know how they managed it without being arrested or reprimanded, but the two of them would prowl the city in a hired wagon and simply lift the youngest urchins off the streets. When they would get back to the orphanage, the soldiers who were stationed at the gates said nothing. Were they shamed into silence, or were they simply glad to see fewer orphans and thus fewer problems?

But since the influx of street urchins had begun, the environment at the orphanage had changed dramatically. The original ten girls and two boys were at a loss as to how to get along with the newcomers. They had been at the orphanage long enough to know how to wait their turn, to ask politely for something, and how to sit in a classroom and learn. The urchins were more like wild animals. Since their parents had been killed a year and a half ago, these children had somehow survived on the streets of Marash through their wits alone. They did not know enough to bathe themselves, or to use a lavatory. If they were hungry, they would simply walk into the kitchen and take what they wanted. The same was true with clothing, blankets, or personal items that the original orphans had somehow managed to acquire. Their lack of discipline played havoc at the complex.

Sarah Baji had always done her utmost to stretch her meager food supplies so that each child would receive adequate nourishment, but now she would walk into her kitchen and find all the figs or her precious hoard of sugar gone. Once, she came in as one of the urchins was making off with a huge bowl of bread dough.

The worst of the bunch was Hrag. He had lived by his wits for so long that it was impossible to know his age, although he couldn't have been older than eight or nine. Like so many of the others, his limbs had been covered with infected scabs when he arrived, and he had been swarming with lice. The first order of the day had been a lice bath, head shave, and new clothing. Marta could not help with the lice baths. Lice carried typhus, and Nurse Bowley was adamant that Marta and her unborn babe stay safe. But she had brought him his new clothing after he'd bathed. As she had handed the items to him with a smile, he had flashed her a look of pure hatred.

"You are a Turkish whore," he had said, spitting on the ground as he grabbed the shirt and trousers from her.

Marta had gasped.

"Look at you," he had said, pointing to her abdomen. "That's a Turk in your belly, isn't it?"

Nurse Bowley had pulled Hrag aside. "Son," she'd said in her stilted Armenian. "Miss Marta is a refugee here just like you are."

"She's a Turkish whore," he had said again, struggling to get out of Nurse Bowley's grasp. Then he had clenched his fists as if to hit Marta. "It's true, isn't it?"

Marta had backed away, holding her arms over her belly. Tears had spilled from her eyes. Then she'd turned and walked away.

"That's right, whore!" Hrag had called after her. "Run away from the truth!"

The next day, when Marta had walked through the orphanage complex to the dining hall, several urchins had walked behind her, pulling at her skirt and grabbing at her abdomen. "It's the Turkish whore!" they'd called. "Here's the Turkish baby!"

Marta's face had burned with embarrassment, but she'd walked on.

It was after this incident that Mr. Brighton had stepped in. He'd tried to rationalize with Hrag and the others, but it was like reasoning with a pack of wolves.

So he'd resolved the problem by designating her dormitory building as a refuge for the girls and women who would have been rescued from Turkish homes. Marta's dormitory building was now labeled the "Rescue Home for Girls" and it was off bounds to all of the street urchins. As of the moment, she was the only "rescued girl," but Mr. Brighton had plans to actually go into Turkish homes and rescue Armenian women. Marta gasped at the audacity of it all. She also wondered whether some of the women would rather not be rescued.

Marta herself had gratefully adapted back to Armenian ways so it galled her to be thought of as Turkish. But she could sympathize with the urchins and realized that many of them had suffered unspeakably at the hands of Turks, so it would take them some time to heal from their traumas. She was loathe to cause them more pain so had agreed to sequester herself in the Rescue Home for the time being. Mr. Brighton had also pointed out that the building would be a good place for Marta to rest in privacy, now that the birth of her child was imminent.

Being in the solitude of the Rescue Home had given Marta

time to accept her situation. She no longer agonized over what anyone thought of her, not even Kevork. She had become pragmatic. Either Kevork was dead or he was alive. If he was dead, at least she would have this baby to love. If he was alive, he could choose to accept her for who she was and what she had suffered through. And she decided that her baby would be the test of his love. If Kevork could not accept her baby, then she would not accept him. Simple to say, but she didn't know how that would play out in real life, if she ever got the chance. There was just one thing certain in her life right now, and that was the baby kicking in her belly.

She accepted that her baby was half Turkish, but its heart was all Armenian. She would name the baby Hovsep, after her father.

The baby kicked again and Marta rubbed her belly tenderly, feeling the curve of her child's heel with the palm of her hand. "I'm glad that Idris brought us here," she murmured lovingly. "This way, you can be all mine."

From her chair by the window in the Rescue Home, Marta was a fair distance from the entrance, but when she craned her head just so, she could see the orphanage gates. Mostly, when they opened, it was for another wagonload of orphans—dirty, ragged, and starving. It broke her heart to see so many, but then again, they were alive.

Just then, the gates opened. But this time it was a horse-drawn carriage instead of a wagon that pulled in and stopped in front of Mr. Brighton's office. A man stepped out of the carriage, and then he steadied the hand of a tall and willowy woman as she too stepped down. She was covered from head to toe in a dark blue chador, and the bottom half of her face was covered with a yellow yashmak. Then came a little girl. Marta squinted to get a better look. She was too young for a chador, so Marta could see the pale blue tunic reaching just below the knees and dark green trousers peeking through underneath. Their faces were a blur at this distance.

Marta gasped. Could it really be her sister? The man was definitely Rustem, the Turk who had been in love with her sister for as long as she could remember. And the little girl had to be Parantzim, the orphan that Mariam and Rustem had adopted. But what were they doing at the orphanage? Marta craned her neck to get a better view.

She wanted to run out, to greet them, but the gates were open. The authorities couldn't know she was here.

A group of ragged Armenian boys clustered around the carriage, shouting at the new arrivals. Marta's heart sank. No! she thought. Please don't hurt them! Hrag picked up a rock. Marta gasped as he threw it at Parantzim, hitting her on the side of the face. When Rustem picked up the little girl and clasped her protectively to his chest, Marta could feel a lump of sadness rise in her throat. Had he grown to love Parantzim as a daughter? Then why was he bringing her back here? But even as she formed the question, she knew the answer. Love was difficult to nurture when straddled between two warring cultures.

The carriage departed, and the orphanage gates closed again. Mr. Brighton led the new arrivals to Marta's building. Marta heard voices at the door. She turned as it clicked open. The willowy woman stood there, removing the yashmak from her face. Marta's heart skipped a beat.

It *was* her sister.

Marta saw the recognition in Mariam's face. But as Mariam's gaze dropped to Marta's enormous belly, the look of joy was replaced by sorrow.

Marta pushed herself from the chair and walked clumsily toward Mariam. The sisters hugged; the bulge of baby squeezed between them. Marta could feel the tears well up into her throat.

How many times had she dreamed of seeing her sister again, only to wake and find that it wasn't true? But here she was—alive. She didn't want to let her go.

"Let me look at you," said Marta. She stepped back, still holding her sister by the arm. With one light fingertip, she traced the outline of her sister's cheek and lips. They were the same, although the lips held a sad firmness about them and the cheeks were pale. She looked into her sister's eyes and realized that they were outlined in kohl, in the Turkish way. And her brows had been darkened with henna. Was Miss Younger right? Had Mariam become a Muslim?

Mariam had always been a beauty, but now she was breathtaking. Marta ran her fingertip down her sister's shoulder and arm until she reached her hand, then she brought the palm of her sister's hand to her lips and kissed it gently. It held a light scent of olive oil. When Marta turned her sister's hand over, she saw the faint traces of an intricate hennaed latticework pattern adorning the back of her sister's hand like a fingerless glove. Marta brought it back up to her lips and kissed it again.

Behind her sister, the little girl was standing silently, her head bowed and her hands at her side. Marta let go of her sister and crouched as best she could so she was nearly eye level with the girl. "Welcome," she said, holding out her hand. "Do you remember me?"

The child looked at Marta's hand but didn't raise her own. There was scratch on her cheek from the rock that had been thrown at her, but it hadn't drawn blood. The girl's eyes were pooled with angry tears.

"I know who you are," said the girl with a touch of coldness in her voice. "You are one of those bad Armenians who were supposed to die in the desert."

Marta heard a small intake of breath from her sister. "You are also Armenian, Parantzim," said Mariam.

"Don't call me that," said the little girl. "My name is Sheruk-rey-ah."

Marta looked from one to the other and sighed. The girl had been successfully indoctrinated.

"I am Turkish now," said Parantzim, her fists clenching. Then her eyes darted around the room, as if looking for a place to hide. But there was no suitable hiding place. A row of thin-mattressed beds stood to the left, with bedrolls neatly stacked at the foot of each. To the right was a long wooden dining table that doubled as a workspace. A packing box sat beside it, overflowing with clothing items donated from abroad. On top of the table were shoes, shirts, trousers, and skirts, sorted into haphazard piles. Sheruk-rey-ah's legs crumpled beneath her and she sat down hard. She wrapped her arms around her knees and bent her head down, as if in shame.

Marta regarded the sad girl on the floor. Then she turned to her sister. "We have much to talk about," she said.

❧ ✦ ☙

That night, Mariam pulled the rough cotton sheets up to her neck and closed her eyes, but she knew that sleep would be long in coming. She was so full of conflicting emotions that her heart felt like it would burst. From the narrow cot beside her, she could hear the muffled sound of Sheruk-rey-ah sobbing into her pillow. Mariam willed herself to stay where she was, not to go and comfort the girl. Hadn't she saved her life earlier today? Sheruk-rey-ah had to toughen up.

Mariam opened her eyes, then turned her head in the direction of the cot on the other side of her. In the semi-darkness, she could see the silhouette of her sister, looking more like the hump of a camel than a sleeping teenaged girl. The details of Marta's pregnancy had been told in hushed exchanges between the sisters when young Sheruk-rey-ah was not listening. Marta had whispered how she and Kevork had been marched into the Syrian Desert at the point of a bayonet. She had whispered details about how Kevork had tried to save her life and her fears that he may have paid with his own. In cold detail, she had told Mariam how she'd escaped death but suffered a worse fate. Mariam had hugged her sister tight and told her that it wasn't her fault. She should feel no guilt.

Guilt.

That was an emotion Mariam knew all about. Mariam's heart was full of guilty little secrets.

Just then, Mariam heard her sister gasp. Mariam threw her covers off and was at her sister's side in a flash. "Are you all right?" she asked.

"My bed is soaked," said Marta, panic in her voice. "I think the baby is coming."

Mariam had witnessed a birth only once before. While in the harem, one of Rustem's father's junior wives had given birth. Mariam and the other women had stood around the bed as witnesses. Mariam remembered sitting and waiting with the other women, eating sweets and making small talk. The junior wife had writhed with pain, but the harem women had pretended not to hear the screams and groans. This had lasted all day and into the night. When the baby had finally come out, the women had exclaimed how ugly the baby was and how unfortunate the mother was to give birth to such a terrible child. This had been said to fool the evil eye into not bothering with the new mother and child. But the details of her labor? Nothing.

"Is there a midwife at the orphanage?" asked Mariam.

"There is an American nurse," said Marta. "Please get her!"

Mariam didn't have to ask where the nurse could be found. She would be in the missionaries' compound. This orphanage had been home to her before the deportations and she knew the layout like the back of her hand. She stood up and pulled her Turkish housedress over her undergarments, then wrapped herself into her chador and ran for the door. Her hand barely touched the handle when she realized that she could not go out of the building dressed as she was. Even though it was night, the sight of her dressed in Turkish clothing would traumatize any orphan who might still be awake. She pulled off the chador in one swift movement. "Is there something I can wear?"

Marta tried to speak, but no words came out: another contraction had just begun and a wave of pain engulfed her. She pointed toward a large wooden box shoved up against the wall beside the wash stand. Mariam ran to it and opened it up. She pulled out a white blouse and a plain black skirt like the missionary women wore. She threw them on and, not bothering with sandals or shoes, flew out the door.

Marta sighed with relief as the door slammed shut behind her sister. Help would be here soon. She tried to breathe slowly. She tried to relax.

Marta hadn't realized she was in labor when it had started. After all, she had never done this before. But the baby was so big that he was pushing up against her back, making it ache. For the last several weeks, every time she'd tried to eat something, she had felt like the food was being pushed back up her throat.

Yesterday morning, she'd noticed a feeling in her womb like a fist tightening then loosening. She had thought maybe it was from sitting and sorting the donated clothing for too long. When the spasms of tightness became more frequent, she had chalked it up to the excitement of seeing Mariam. It wasn't until she had tried to get to sleep that the rhythm of the tightening womb became more intense. At first, she'd tried to ignore it, but when the contractions came closer and closer together, sleep had been no longer possible. What would she have done if Mariam hadn't come back to the orphanage when she did?

"Does it hurt?"

Marta looked up and saw Sheruk-rey-ah standing there, still wearing her Turkish-style tunic and trousers. The little girl's eyes were round with fear.

"A little bit," said Marta, grimacing bravely.

Sheruk-rey-ah tentatively reached out her hand and patted Marta's forehead. "You're hot," she said. Then she walked to the basin and dipped a small towel into the pitcher of water and wrung it out so that it was just damp. She brought it back and draped it over Marta's forehead.

Marta gripped the little girl's hand. "Thank you, dear."

The loving gesture brought back memories of another Parantzim: Marta's own mother. Once, when she was little, Marta had had a fever that lasted all night. Her mother had sat by her bedside, bathing her body with a cool damp cloth. She swallowed back a sob. Her mother had been dead for so long; these memories were precious.

"Do you remember your mother, Sheruk-rey-ah?" Marta asked. The Turkish name stuck on her lips, but she respected the girl's choice.

The little girl shook her head. "I don't remember anything from before," the girl said in a small voice. "The first thing I remember is when Rustem Bey and Mariam came to the orphanage in their fine carriage and brought me back to the harem."

"Don't you remember me?" asked Marta.

The girl looked at her intently for a moment before speaking. "I remember your face," said Sheruk-rey-ah. "But I don't know why."

It was no wonder the little girl had blocked so much from her memory. No doubt she had witnessed her parents' execution only hours before showing up at the orphanage gates, just before the deportations began. And then she would have witnessed the rounding up of all the Armenian adults at the orphanage. Sometimes it was easier to forget.

"I was happy at Rustem Bey's house," said the girl.

Marta nodded, glad to have any conversation that took her mind off the rhythm of the shooting pain in her back.

"Rustem is a good man," said Marta. She thought back to all of the times Rustem Bey would come to the orphanage with a cartload of food. He was paid for it, but no more than what he would have got had he sold the goods to Turks. Most merchants had stopped supplying food to the orphanage in the week or two before the deportations. Miss Younger had come to depend on Rustem more and more. Marta knew that Rustem didn't hate Armenians and he didn't blame Armenians the way that many Turks did. She also knew that he had fallen in love with her sister.

"Did you know that Rustem asked Mariam to marry him and she said no?" said Sheruk-rey-ah as she turned the towel so the cooler side touched Marta's forehead.

So they *hadn't* got married. Miss Younger had been wrong. "Is that why you two came back here?" she asked Sheruk-rey-ah.

"No," said the girl. "That was long ago. I don't know why we suddenly had to leave. I was so happy there."

Marta turned her head and looked into the girl's eyes. A single tear was rolling down her cheek. Marta reached out and squeezed Sheruk-rey-ah's hand. "It may not feel like it," Marta said, "but my sister did this for your safety."

"I don't believe you," the girl said.

Sixteen

MARTA AND MARIAM

As Mariam ran breathlessly toward the missionaries' compound, she marveled at how odd this clothing felt. She could feel the breeze on her uncovered face and she liked how it whipped through her hair. But the western-styled skirt and blouse was not nearly as comfortable as her loose long Turkish tunic and pants. The skirt cinched at her waist and bunched at her ankles, making it hard for her to run.

When she got to the missionaries' quarters, she banged on the door with her fist. It was probably only minutes, but it seemed like hours when the door finally opened. Mr. Brighton stood there in a night robe, his hair mussed and his monocle askew.

"Marta is having the baby," she said.

"Already?" Mr. Brighton's eyes widened at the news. "I'll wake Nurse Bowley."

Moments later, he reappeared, this time accompanied by a small woman who was dressed in a white blouse and black skirt just like Mariam's. She carried a black leather satchel. She nodded to Mariam and said, "Let's get going."

Even though the woman looked like she was walking, she moved so quickly that Mariam had trouble keeping up with her. When they got to the Rescue Home for Girls, Nurse Bowley barreled in, Mariam right behind her.

Marta had propped herself up to a sitting position in the bed. There was a look of panic in her eyes. "I'm all wet...down there," she said.

"Never mind, dear," said Nurse Bowley. "Your water just broke. You're in good hands, so relax."

Not as easy as it sounds, thought Marta, who was suffering incredible waves of pain. Nurse Bowley took it in stride. "It is part of being a woman," she said. "Soon it will be over, and you will hold your baby in your arms."

The nurse ordered Mariam to fetch some fresh water for boiling, then she turned to Sheruk-rey-ah.

"Dear," she said, "could you put your hands on Marta's lower back and gently push? That will be most helpful."

Sheruk-rey-ah set down the damp cloth and perched herself on the bed beside Marta. "Would you like me to push right here?" she asked, gingerly placing both of her hands on the small of Marta's back.

Marta groaned and nodded in appreciation.

There was a storage room off to one side of the sleeping quarters that contained extra furniture and bedding. Nurse Bowley walked over to it and pulled out some items, then she dragged out a contraption that looked like an angled high-backed wooden chair with a frame instead of a seat. She pushed it to the foot of Marta's bed.

"What's that?" asked Marta, pointing to the contraption.

"A birthing chair," said the nurse. "Now let me see how you're coming along."

Sheruk-rey-ah removed her hands from Marta's back and stepped away. Marta gingerly rolled onto her back.

Nurse Bowley folded the blanket up from the bottom half of Marta's body and then she sat down at the end of the bed. "Marta, can you put your feet on either side of the bed and open your knees so I can see how the baby is progressing?"

Marta did as she was told.

"All right," said the nurse. "I am going to put my fingers in to measure how far along you are. Breathe in, dear, then breath out slowly. Not much happening yet."

Just then, another wave of pain engulfed Marta. She clutched the mattress and groaned. "It feels like a lot to me," she panted.

"You're only one finger dilated," said Nurse Bowley. "It's going to be a long night. You should try to rest, and I am going to do the same. I will be back in two hours."

Once Nurse Bowley left, Mariam grabbed a chair from the other room and set it down beside her sister. "I am here, my dear," she said, reaching for Marta's hand. "You're going to be fine."

Marta gripped Mariam's hand with all her might. Despite the pain, it was wonderful to have a sister. It was so good not to be alone anymore. Another wave of contractions engulfed her. Marta winced with pain and took shallow panting breaths.

"Breathe slowly," said Mariam soothingly. She let go of her sister's hand and sat down on the edge of the bed. Then Marta felt her sister's warm hands firmly but gently massage the small of her back. She willed herself to breathe slowly. In, one two three four five six. Out, one two three four five six. Relax, relax, relax.

She could feel her sister's breath on her neck. "Tell me about how you came to be at Rustem Bey's house," she said. Maybe the story would take her mind off her pain. And they had all night, didn't they?

Mariam pushed herself farther onto Marta's bed so that she could sit more comfortably while applying pressure to her sister's back. Sheruk-rey-ah sat down on the bed beside Marta's.

"Can I listen to the story too?" she asked.

Mariam nodded. "You remember the day when the deportations started?" she began.

How could she forget? For six years, they'd lived and thrived at the orphanage, almost managing to put behind them the sadness of their parents' deaths in the Adana Massacre of 1909.

Kevork had just proposed too. Rustem Bey, whose father's company was a regular supplier for the orphanage, had fallen in love with Mariam, but she had no interest in marrying a Muslim.

On that morning in April 1915, it was clear and dry. The sun was hot, and dust swirled in the courtyard when the gates opened. Captain Sayyid, who was in charge of the Turkish Army in Marash, entered on his signature white horse.

All two hundred children had formed neat rows on the ground, sitting on their bedrolls. Marta, Mariam, Kevork, and the other older orphans, were in the front row. The missionaries and teachers stood off to one side. They were all rigid with fear. The captain's reputation for cruelty was legendary.

Captain Sayyid got off his horse and strode in front of the children, inspecting them one by one. He deemed all the older orphans as adults. They could no longer count on refuge in the orphanage. They were to be marched out into the desert with all of the other adult Armenians in Marash.

"If it had been my fate to join you and Kevork, who was like a brother to me, I would have accepted it," said Mariam. "We would have been together. But Captain Sayyid reserved a special fate for me. I was forced up behind him onto his horse. When the gates closed behind us, that part of my life ended.

"He took me to an auction house for slaves," said Mariam. "I was stripped and examined like an animal, then auctioned off to the highest bidder. Rustem somehow got wind of what was happening, and he got there and managed to purchase me."

"You were fortunate," said Marta. "Rustem has always been a good friend."

"Yes he has," agreed Mariam.

"Then why wouldn't you marry him?" asked Sheruk-rey-ah.

"You don't marry everyone who is your friend, do you?" responded Mariam chidingly to the girl.

"I would marry him if he asked me," said Sheruk-rey-ah.

Mariam sighed, then continued with her story.

"He also bought Ani Topalian."

Marta looked up. "*The* Ani Topalian?" she asked in surprise. The Topalian family had been one of the wealthiest in all of Marash.

"Yes," said Mariam. "It was the Topalian family home that had been turned into an auction house."

Marta sighed. "If any Armenian family could have bought their way to safety, it was the Topalians."

"The rich were the first targets," said Mariam. She paused for a moment. "Sheruk-rey-ah, could you massage Marta's back for a bit? My hands are getting sore."

The two switched positions and Mariam continued with her story.

"Rustem took both of us back to his father's harem. Ani's parents had been friends with Rustem's parents for years, and so she was welcome. I was not so welcome."

"Why not?" asked Marta.

"Rustem's mother thought that I had designs on her son. Nothing could have been further from the truth! She did everything in her power to make it uncomfortable for me."

"And that's why we had to leave," said Sheruk-rey-ah in a pouting voice.

"Hardly," said Mariam dryly.

"Did Rustem treat you well?" asked Marta.

"Very well, gentleman that he is," said Mariam wistfully. "He looked after my every need and treated me with respect. He even let me go back to the orphanage to rescue this young lady." She pointed to Sheruk-rey-ah.

"I had to pose as his concubine to do it, but we came back and Rustem formally adopted Parantz—Sheruk-rey-ah."

"There were almost no orphans left by then," said Sheruk-rey-ah. "People kept on coming in and taking them. I didn't understand what was happening."

Mariam knew, but she didn't want to say in front of the child.

"I was so happy at Rustem Bey's house," the girl said, her voice trembling with emotion. "I still don't understand why we had to leave."

Mariam looked at Sheruk-rey-ah with anger. "You really don't understand, do you?"

"No," said the girl, sticking out her bottom lip in a pout. "I had candy there, and toys. And beautiful clothing."

"Do you remember Ani?" asked Mariam.

"Of course," said Sheruk-rey-ah. "We played together every day until Rustem's mother sent her to Canada."

"Sheruk-rey-ah," said Mariam. "It is time that you know the truth." Mariam paused for a moment, as if to gather strength for what she had to say. "Rustem's mother did not send her to Canada."

"Then where is she?" asked Sheruk-rey-ah.

"Dead," said Mariam. "She developed a cough. A minor thing really, but Rustem's mother decided Ani was too much trouble, so she ordered her neck wrung."

"No!" cried Sheruk-rey-ah. "You lie!" She stood up from the bed, balled her hands into fists, and swung them at Mariam.

Mariam caught the girl by the wrists and tried to hug her, but Sheruk-rey-ah broke free.

"Rustem told me himself," said Mariam, her voice trembling with emotion. "And it was Rustem who decided that you and I had to leave that instant. For our own safety."

"It's not true," cried Sheruk-rey-ah. Then she ran from the room.

⤜✝⤛

Mariam wanted to go and comfort Sheruk-rey-ah when she ran off, but she didn't. Better for the child to think this through on her own, she reasoned. Time was the best healer.

"Poor Ani," said Marta. "How could a gentle soul like Rustem Bey have such a brutal mother?"

"That is a question I have often asked myself," said Mariam. "And I respect him even more, knowing the steep price he has paid for helping the Armenians. He has lost his family."

"And poor Sheruk-rey-ah," said Marta. "What a shock for her."

"She was a little bit too fond of the luxury in the harem," said Mariam. "She seemed not to realize that she was no more important than a stray kitten there—" Mariam's voice choked into a sob. "I wish I had known in time. It is my fault that Ani is dead."

Marta pushed herself onto her other side, trying to find a comfortable position. "Sit down here," she said to Mariam, patting the side of the bed.

Mariam sat. Marta reached for her hand and gave it a reassuring squeeze. "You did everything you could," she said.

"But I feel so guilty," said Mariam. "If only I could have saved her—" then her voice dissolved in a torrent of tears.

"It is fine, it is fine," cooed Marta. She squeezed her sister's hand comfortingly, oblivious for a short time of the increasing intensity of her own rhythmic contractions. Then all at once, a contraction became so intense that she gasped in pain.

Abruptly, Mariam's tears stopped. She roughly dried her face with the back of her hand. "I am sorry," she said to Marta. "Here I am, being comforted by you when you are the one in need of comfort." She took a deep shuddering gulp of air and willed her tears away. She dried her face with her skirt and then gently massaged her sister's back.

><~÷~<

Hours later, Mariam heard a shuffling sound in the doorway. "Mariam…," said a small voice. She looked up. Sheruk-rey-ah stood there, eyes brimming with tears. The resentful look, which had been on her face since their abrupt departure from the harem, was gone. In its place was an expression of sorrow. "Thank you, Mariam," was all the girl said.

Mariam stood up and took a step toward the girl. Sheruk-rey-ah ran toward her, then wrapped her arms around her waist, hugging her with all her might. Mariam could feel the wracking sobs course through the girl's body.

"You're safe now, dear," she cooed. She kneeled and pulled the girl onto her lap. "I am sorry that I couldn't save Ani."

><~÷~<

The door creaked open in the wee hours before morning and Nurse Bowley stepped in. By this time, Sheruk-rey-ah had fallen into an exhausted sleep on one of the beds. Mariam was perched on the side of Marta's bed.

Marta looked up with relief and gave the nurse a grateful smile.

The nurse checked her again. "You're progressing," she said. "It won't be long now."

After what seemed like hours, Marta felt a change in the contractions. "I need to push," she gasped.

Nurse Bowley checked her again. "You're five fingers dilated. The baby is ready to be born." She took Marta's hands and gently helped her to her feet and over to the chair.

Marta sat down gingerly on it, resting her hands on the armrests, expecting that the position of the chair would relieve the pressure and the urge to push, but it didn't.

"I must push!" she cried.

"That's the idea," the nurse answered. She got the washbasin from the stand and placed it on the floor underneath the chair. Then she sat on a stool in front of the chair, which was angled in such a way that she could see everything that was happening.

"Push. Now!"

Mariam stood beside her sister and gripped one of her hands. Sheruk-rey-ah had woken up abruptly. Rubbing sleep out of her eyes, she got up and stood beside Mariam.

Marta pushed with all her strength. Her insides felt like they were being stretched beyond possibility.

"I can see the top of the baby's head!" cried Nurse Bowley. "It's crowning!"

Sheruk-rey-ah stepped closer to the nurse so she could see what was happening.

Mariam reached over so she could hold both of her sister's hands in hers. "It will be over soon, Marta."

Just then, the head of the baby emerged. One more big push. Marta watched as the baby emerged from between her legs. The nurse caught the baby. Mariam handed Nurse Bowley a clean boiled cloth. The nurse wiped away the blood and a white waxy substance from the baby's nose and mouth. The baby's face contorted and out of the tiny lips came a lusty howl.

Sheruk-rey-ah grimaced.

"My son," said Marta. "My dear Hovsep…"

"Your daughter," said Nurse Bowley, glancing up briefly.

"A daughter?" cried Marta. "Then I shall name her Parantzim, after my mother."

Her baby was perfect. And she watched with awe the blood that pulsed through the umbilical cord, giving her blood to her daughter.

An image flashed in her brain: the last time she had seen Parantzim, her mother. The slit across her throat. All that blood.

At last, the pulsing stopped. Nurse Bowley cut the cord. Mariam handed her a piece of boiled cotton that had been ripped into a strip and the nurse tied off the cord. Then she handed the baby to Mariam.

"You need to push one more time, Marta," said Nurse Bowley. "The afterbirth needs to come out."

Marta pushed with all of the strength that she could muster, and the placenta slipped out and into the basin. The nurse examined her carefully to make sure that nothing was left inside, and then she placed a clean cloth between Marta's legs. She took the baby from Mariam. "Help your sister back into the bed, dear," she said.

Then Nurse Bowley washed the baby and wrapped her in a white cotton cloth. She placed the baby gently in Marta's arms.

Marta gazed intently into her baby's face. She feared that she would see the facial features of the Turk whose third wife she had unwillingly become. She stared at the baby's dimpled chin and angry red cheeks and tiny lips forming the *O* of a howl. For a moment the baby did look like that man—on those days when anger consumed him and he would beat her within an inch of her life. But then she closed her eyes and banished the image. This baby would have a new life. She would be untainted from the hatred of the past.

She looked up at Nurse Bowley. "What is the English name for Parantzim?" she asked.

"Pauline," said Nurse Bowley with a smile. "A lovely name."

"Pauline," whispered Marta to herself. It seemed right. It was still her mother's name, but it was new and fresh and had no blood on it.

A tear rolled from her cheek. She opened her eyes and saw that the tear had landed on her baby's forehead. "Pauline," whispered Marta. "My dear Pauline." Marta lightly formed the sign of the cross with the tear onto her daughter's brow. She looked at her baby's lips and cheeks and eyes, and she banished all thoughts of the man who raped her. She willed herself to see the image of her mother while she was alive and happy and loving.

She opened her robe and brought Pauline to her breast.

Nurse Bowley stripped Marta's bloodied bedding off the mattress and tied it into a bundle. She remade the bed with freshly laundered sheets. Then she held little Pauline while Mariam helped her sister strip out of her soiled sleeping tunic. When she finished washing, Marta donned a long roomy tunic and gratefully crawled into the newly made bed.

Nurse Bowley looked down at the beautiful baby in her arms. Pauline's eyes were closed and her face was peaceful, but her fists were clenched tight, as if ready to defend herself.

Marta propped herself up on one elbow and reached out with the other hand. "Let me cuddle her," she said. Nurse Bowley lay the baby down beside her mother. Marta wrapped one arm around her daughter and sighed with satisfaction.

"Do you want me to help you with those?" Mariam asked, pointing to the bundle of bloodied bedding and clothing.

"Get your sleep," answered Nurse Bowley. "I can carry this to the laundry on my own."

Mariam nodded gratefully. She was tired to the bone. But before she went back to bed, she needed to find Sheruk-rey-ah. The little girl was not in any of the cots in the dormitory, nor had she fallen asleep on the floor beside one of the beds. Mariam walked out in the dining area and found the child asleep at the long dining table, her head slumped in her arms, and a pile of sorted clothing in front of her. The girl still wore her Turkish-style tunic and trousers, although they were now creased and sweaty.

Mariam tapped Sheruk-rey-ah gently on the shoulder.

The girl didn't move. Mariam bent down and tucked one arm under the girl's knees and another around her back. She lifted her up and carried her to the dormitory bed on the other side of Mariam's. Gently she set the child down, covering her with a blanket.

Mariam crawled into her own bed. She was asleep before her head hit the pillow.

Marta watched her sister carry in Sheruk-rey-ah and tuck her into the bed. It warmed her heart to see Mariam give so much love to a child who wasn't hers by blood. She looked down at her own beautiful sleeping baby. With a touch as light as a feather, she traced Pauline's nose, lips, and forehead with her fingertip. Pauline wrinkled her nose in acknowledgment but didn't waken. If Kevork lived, would he be able to love this child as much as Mariam loved Sheruk-rey-ah? She could only hope. She drifted off to a peaceful sleep.

Marta dreamed of her mother yet again. Parantzim was at the foot of her bed, tears streaming down her face. "Get up. Hide," she said, urgently. "Pauline is in danger."

Marta sat up like a bolt. It was not yet dawn. Pauline's face was twisted into an angry *O*, and her swaddling was soaked through with urine. She picked up the baby and took her over to the basin. She lay Pauline down on the dresser top and began to unwrap her. Marta looked frantically around the room for fresh lengths of cotton.

Mariam sat up in bed, roused by baby's cries. "What is it you need?" she asked.

"Fresh swaddling cotton," said Marta.

Mariam got up and found a neatly folded pile of freshly ripped strips of cotton resting on the bed on the other side of Marta's. She reached for one set and brought it to her sister.

"I will hold her feet up and you unwind the cloth," said Marta, grateful for her sister's help. Sheruk-rey-ah had awakened by this time too. She stood on her toes beside Mariam and watched the proceedings.

Pauline continued to cry as the two sisters unwrapped the cloth. Sheruk-rey-ah wrinkled her nose in disgust. But she continued watching.

Marta dunked a clean cloth into the basin of water and cleaned her daughter as best she could. Then the two sisters tried to swaddle Pauline in the same way that Nurse Bowley had done. But Pauline was kicking her legs and crying at the top of her tiny lungs, so it was a futile effort.

"I think you need to feed her first," said Mariam.

Marta gathered the struggling naked baby into her arms and took her back to the bed. She opened her tunic and drew the baby to her breast, but Pauline was crying in frantic gulps and didn't seem to know what to do. Finally Marta directed her nipple into the baby's mouth and Pauline latched on. The baby's limbs relaxed, and then she sucked.

Mariam draped a blanket over her sister's shoulders and around Pauline too. She gathered up the dirty swaddling clothes and tied them in a bundle.

Just then, there was a pounding at the door. It reminded Marta of her frightening dream. Was Pauline in danger? She looked down, but Pauline was so content that she hadn't even flinched at the sound.

Mariam ran to the door and opened it a crack. It was Mr. Brighton.

"I am terribly sorry to disturb you at such an hour," he said hurriedly. "But you must hide. The Turkish authorities will be arriving at dawn to deport you both."

Seventeen

KEVORK

Several months had passed by the time Kevork got back to Aleppo and Miss Schultz. He was tired to the bone with aching muscles and itchy with lice when he pulled the rope on the familiar bell. She opened the gate wide at the sight of him and pulled him in.

She wrinkled her nose at his dirty clothing. Kevork saw her take note of the healed lesions on his face and hands. He knew she realized he'd had typhus, but she said nothing about it.

"First a bath," she said. "Then food, and we can talk."

He followed her through the dusty courtyard and was going to follow her inside the house when she held up her hands. "Stay here," she said.

She opened the door and whistled. An older Armenian boy ran up to the doorway. Kevork marveled at how healthy he looked. He was dressed in a simple cotton shirt and trousers, and his hair was cut close to the scalp. He had no open sores and no lice, and his eyes sparkled with intelligence.

"Bring the wash tub out here, Razmig, and fill it with water," she said to the boy. "Get Garabed to help you."

The boy grinned and ran back inside.

"No one with lice enters," explained Miss Schultz. "So the first bath is always in the courtyard."

As Kevork waited for the boys to fill the tub with pails of water, he stripped off his clothing. Razmig gathered the clothing up and carried it to a metal contraption that was set up in the courtyard. It had two small wheels at the back with a tublike reservoir above it, and two large wheels at the front, supporting something that looked like a smokestack.

Razmig threw Kevork's clothing into the contraption's reservoir and then poked at it with a long stick. He looked amused at Kevork's confusion. "This is a delouser," he explained.

It seemed to work by either smoking or fuming the lice to death. What Sister Helena would have given for a contraption like that! Much of the deportees' clothing at Meskene had to be burned to stop the lice infestations.

Despite the cold water and lack of privacy, Kevork relished in scrubbing every last bit of dirt from under his fingernails and between his toes. He rubbed the bar of soap through his hair and then lathered it up, feeling the clusters of lice eggs come loose from his scalp. Razmig passed him a towel as he stepped out onto a woven grass mat. As he dried himself vigorously, he looked back at the dirty water with a grimace. The entire surface of the water was a brown crust of lice. Razmig, obviously used to this, sprinkled a chemical powder on the surface of the water to make sure all of them were dead.

Then he held up a flask of liquid. "I need to pour this over your hair," he said to Kevork. "It's vinegar, to kill the eggs."

Kevork bent down, his eyes shut, and the boy thoroughly soaked every strand of hair from scalp to end.

"Stand back," said Kevork to the boy, then he shook his head back and forth like a wet dog, sending droplets of vinegar through the air.

Razmig took Kevork's robe from the delousing machine,

shook it vigorously, then handed it to Kevork, who slipped it on and belted it, luxuriating in the feeling of cleanliness as he walked up the steps.

He was surprised when he stepped through the door of the orphanage. What used to be an empty room was now filled with rows of wooden benches and countertops. Young girls—thin, hair shorn to the scalp for lice—sat silently in rows with coarse cloths spread out before them on the countertops. They were sewing trousers and tunics by hand.

He stepped into the next room. This one contained eight hospital cots placed close together. Each cot held an emaciated child with wounds that had been cleaned and dressed. Most were asleep, but one little girl's eyes followed Kevork as he left the room and walked through to Miss Schultz's office.

The door was closed, so he tapped on it. "Come in," Miss Schultz called.

Kevork pushed the door open and stepped inside. Her office too had changed. The oriental sofa was cleared and was now placed opposite Miss Schultz. And instead of a plain wooden table, she now sat at a desk. The wooden table was shoved up against one wall and was strewn with papers. Her desktop was also covered with papers.

"Sit down," she said, pointing to the sofa.

Kevork did as he was told. He noticed that she didn't smile at all. She didn't seem happy that he had returned.

Before she could say anything, Kevork spoke up. "Have you heard from Miss Younger about my betrothed?"

Miss Schultz sighed. "No," she said, a blush rising on her cheeks. "I have not heard back."

Kevork hadn't really expected her to find out anything about Marta, but still, the lack of any news was devastating. Sometimes he wondered whether it might be better knowing that she was dead than knowing nothing at all.

"So she could still be alive," said Kevork, more to himself than to Miss Schultz.

"Anything is possible," said Miss Schultz gently. "We can pray that she is still alive."

Kevork nodded, then closed his eyes and willed the tears not to come. He took a deep breath to calm himself and changed the subject. "I distributed all of the money," he told her. "And I got as far as Meskene."

"That is admirable," said Miss Schultz, her voice flat with exhaustion. "And I am pleased that you made it back here safely."

"Do you want me to do another trip?" he asked.

"Not now," she said. "That would be too risky. But we will have another job for you, I am sure."

Kevork nodded. "Where will you find me?" he asked.

"Go back to your rooftop abode," she said. "See if you can reopen your stall at the market. Wait for one of our messengers."

Just then, there was a tap at the door and Razmig stepped in, holding a tray of flat bread and a tall glass of chilled tan.

"Thank you, Razmig," said Miss Schultz. "You can set it down here." She pushed some of the papers on her desk aside to make room for the tray.

"Refresh yourself before you leave," said Miss Schultz. "I am sure you must be hungry."

Kevork ripped off a chunk of bread and shoved it into his mouth. It was fresh and moist and delicious—the best food he had tasted in months. It felt wonderful to be washed, to sit in clean clothing with good food in front of him. But as he chewed, an image of starving children, reaching out, tugging at his robe, appeared in his mind. The bread no longer tasted fresh. It was like wood in his mouth. He tried chewing again, but he almost choked. He sipped some tan to moisten the bread, but the image would not go away. He swallowed the bite with difficulty, then took another sip of the tan to wash down the last bits of bread. He set down the glass. Kevork didn't think he'd ever get pleasure out of eating again. Not as long as there were so many Armenians in deportation camps.

"Thank you for everything you do," said Kevork to Miss Schultz as he stood up.

She stood up too and extended her hand. "Be safe," she said. "And I will get word to you if I hear anything about your Marta."

"Bless you," said Kevork.

"And here are your tools," she said, walking over to the corner of the room and shifting aside packages and boxes stockpiled there. Underneath it all was the cloth-covered package, just as it had been left months before.

Kevork took the tools and placed them back in his rucksack. Then he walked out of the orphanage gates and back through the streets of Aleppo.

Kevork sighed with relief when he rounded the corner and his own familiar door came into view. But when he pushed it open and entered, he was appalled to see that the girls were gone. The looms were also gone. The room was empty, save for a single, half-made carpet in green that had been slashed and torn from its loom. Where was Angele?

He walked over to the damaged carpet. The color and the distinctive sunburst pattern was a sign of her work. He took the knife from his rucksack and cut the carpet piece free of its tangled bits of yarn. Then he folded it up and tucked it under his arm. He looked around to see if there was anything there that would give him a clue about where she was taken, but there was no other sign of Angele or the other girls.

He ran up the earthen steps to his own abode and was shocked to see that his small makeshift table had been knocked over and his tent had been ripped in half. It had obviously been a raid to round up more Armenians. Where would they have taken Angele and the girls? He was afraid even to think of what she might be going through right now. He was about to leave when he noticed a small fluttering of something gray sticking out of a crack in the wall. It was a rock dove's feather. At first he was confused, but then he understood. He was sure that it was a message from Angele. *Go to the boy who loves birds.*

Kevork wrapped the square of sunburst carpet into his prayer mat and shoved them both in his rucksack. He hurried down the steps and out the door. He didn't want to go directly to Zeki's house in case he was being followed, so he went to the market. He wanted to see if someone else had taken over his stall, but when he got there, he saw soldiers at the entrance. He turned away, not wanting to go in.

He wandered up and down the cobbled streets in no particular direction, just to be certain that no one was following him. After an hour or more of mindless meandering, he headed toward Zeki's house.

When he arrived, he was disturbed to see a crowd of people standing outside. He was about to leave when he stopped long enough to hear what they were saying. They were all patients of Zeki's father. The waiting room was too full, and they had lined up outside.

"Go in," said one of the men to him in Arabic. "If they don't take down your name, you will be waiting all day."

So Kevork walked in. The waiting room was filled with men of all ages. One man had brought a goat with him, and another a chicken. Kevork assumed that this was in payment for treatment.

Kevork walked up to the secretary, who sat behind a desk. He was extremely fat and wore a red fez, an ivory-colored tunic, and brown trousers. He was busily writing in a ledger with a quill pen. The secretary looked up when Kevork approached.

"You're here to see the surgeon?" the secretary asked him in a bored tone of voice.

"Yes," said Kevork.

"How will you be paying?" asked the secretary.

"I can pay him in flowers," responded Kevork in a voice barely above a whisper. He hoped that no one else in the waiting room was listening. He could feel his heart thumping in his throat.

The secretary looked up sharply and held Kevork in his gaze. "Yes," he said. "We have been expecting you."

Kevork said nothing. The secretary continued to write for a moment. Then he set down his quill pen. "Follow me," he said to Kevork, opening a door at the far end of the room and stepping through.

As Kevork followed him, he could hear murmurs of discontent from the waiting room. "Why is he getting in so quickly when I have been waiting all day?" someone said. Kevork shrugged apologetically to the waiting patients and shut the door behind him.

The secretary led Kevork past a medicinal-smelling examining room and a small surgical suite. As they walked by, Kevork could see that the suite was occupied. The white drapes were pulled shut, but he could see the silhouette of a patient who was stretched out on a table.

"This way," said the secretary, leading him farther down the corridor. He stopped at a closed mahogany door. "Wait here," he said, then he left Kevork alone.

Kevork stood there, shifting from foot to foot, for half an hour or more. The doctor didn't come out of the surgical suite and no one else approached. Just when Kevork was about to give up, the mahogany door opened, and a woman dressed in a white blouse and teal green long skirt beckoned him in. Her glossy black hair was parted in the middle and braided into a single plait down her back. Neither her eyes nor eyebrows were enhanced with kohl.

"Sit down," she said, motioning with her hand to a high-backed plush chair that was positioned opposite a huge mahogany desk. She walked to the other side of the desk and sat down.

"I am Nisa Hanim, Zeki's mother," said the woman.

Kevork tried to hide his surprise. He had never seen a Turkish woman unveiled and dressed in western clothing. "I...I am Khedive...Kevork, the shoemaker...the courier."

Nisa Hanim smiled at his discomposure. "I know who you are," she said. "I have been expecting you."

"What happened to the girls...the carpet weavers?" asked Kevork.

The smile disappeared from Nisa Hanim's face. "Your Angele is safe," she said. "But the other girls have been taken to Deir Ez Zor."

"My God," said Kevork. He could feel bile rise in his throat. Those poor girls, he thought. They will never survive. "How did it happen?" he asked.

"An informer," whispered Nisa Hanim. She clenched her hands together until her knuckles turned white. "We have lost so many of our safe houses."

"Where is Angele?" asked Kevork.

She held a finger to her lips. "Shhhh," she said. Then she pointed to the floor. "In our basement," she whispered.

"Can I see her?" whispered Kevork. A million thoughts were swirling in his head. How had she managed to escape? How safe would she be here? Where could *he* go, now that his home had been uncovered?

"Of course," said the woman, getting up and walking toward the door. "But not right now."

"When?" asked Kevork, standing up and following.

"Can you come after sunset?" she asked.

"Yes," said Kevork.

"Take the back steps," said Nisa Hanim, pointing to the far end of the corridor. "They take you up to the roof. You can get away without the patients seeing you. Just be back here after sunset prayer. Rap on the door eight times so we know it is you."

Kevork stepped up on to the housetop and hopped from roof to roof until he was far away from the surgeon's house. He sat on one roof for a bit, watching the people down below until his eyes began to droop with exhaustion. Since his illness, he tired easily. He lay down on the flat clay roof of a vacant house and slept.

He was awakened by the sound of a muezzin on a minaret of a nearby mosque, calling the faithful to sunset prayer. As the last rays of sun disappeared behind the Citadel, Kevork climbed down from the rooftop and walked back to the Ayguns' house.

He did not want to approach the house until he knew that all of the patients had left for the day. The street was still busy in front of the surgeon's house, and some soldiers were also milling around. He found a café not far from the doctor's house and waited there. Kevork sipped his coffee and kept his eye on the surgeon's house. He watched with interest as the last patient left. A few minutes later, the fat secretary stepped out through the front door, bowing good-bye to someone inside.

Just for good measure, Kevork continued to wait.

Another half hour passed with no activity at the surgeon's house. Kevork set a coin on the table for his coffee and stood up. As he walked toward the house, through the corner of his eye he could see a Turkish soldier on the other side of the street slightly behind him, walking in the same direction. When Kevork got to the surgeon's house he walked two houses past and ducked into an alleyway. From his hiding place, he watched the soldier stop at the surgeon's door.

Kevork gasped in recognition. It was the same soldier who had come to the market to have his rifle strap repaired. The soldier looked left and right. Kevork ducked. Then the soldier gave the door three firm knocks.

There was no answer. The soldier knocked again and waited, kicking the dirt with his toe in impatience. Still no answer. The soldier grasped the doorknob and tried to turn it, but the door wouldn't open. Kevork watched as the soldier muttered something to himself and stomped off.

Kevork waited in his hiding spot for several more minutes. The soldier was nowhere in sight when he stepped out from the alleyway and walked briskly back to the surgeon's house. He gave the door eight firm raps. The door opened immediately and an arm pulled him in. The door was shut quickly behind him.

An unfamiliar man stood at the threshold beside Nisa Hanim.

"I am Khedive Ayakkabici," said Kevork to the man, bowing deeply.

"Ah, yes. Kevork Khedive," said the man, bowing in return. "And I am Dr. Aygun. You have already met my wife. Come in. We have been expecting you." Then he bolted the door with a metal bar.

Dr. Aygun was not what Kevork had expected. After everything he had heard about this man, Kevork had built an image in his mind that matched the doctor's reputation. But the man who stood before him was slight, nearly bird like in his fragility, and a full head shorter than his wife. He wore a simple white shirt with the sleeves rolled up to the elbow. The shirt billowed on his small frame, and Kevork noticed that extra notches had recently been added to the doctor's leather belt. Dr. Aygun's skin was papery thin and had a faint yellow hue.

"We must talk," said the doctor in a strong voice that belied his physique. Then he and his wife led Kevork away from the waiting room and down the corridor to the office where Kevork had been earlier in the day. Dr. Aygun sat down at the desk, and his wife stood behind him, one hand placed gently on his shoulder.

Kevork was worried about Angele. He had been waiting all day to see for himself that she was all right. But the look on Dr. Aygun's face compelled him to keep his patience and to sit for a moment and listen.

"Angele escaped the raid on her place by running up to the roof and onto a neighboring rooftop," said Dr. Aygun. "They searched the roof, but somehow she managed to evade capture."

"How did you find her?" asked Kevork.

"Our son, Zeki, found her," said Dr. Aygun. "Word came about the betrayal a day after it happened. He went to her place to see for himself. He almost missed her. She was hiding under a half-made carpet."

"But how did you get her here?" asked Kevork. His mind was filled with an image of Angele, alone and afraid, cowering in her hiding place, not knowing what would happen to her next.

"Zeki went back in the early hours of the morning," said the doctor. "He brought some of his old clothing for her to wear. She did not call so much attention to herself dressed like a Turkish street boy with her hair hidden under a cap."

"That was a great risk he took," said Kevork.

"Indeed," said the doctor. "The authorities have become more stringent with their searches, and it is only a matter of time before they uncover our rescue activities."

Kevork's mind was filled with the image of the soldier at their door just moments before. How long would it take him to come back with reinforcements to search the Ayguns' place from top to bottom?

Nisa Hanim said, "We need to make a decision about Angele."

"What do you mean?" asked Kevork.

"We could hide her in a safe Turkish home," said Nisa Hanim. "One that the authorities would never search."

"Where?" asked Kevork.

"With my first cousin," explained Nisa Hanim. "We have managed to place a few lucky Armenian girls amongst trusted friends and family. Neither the police nor the army has female officers, and harems are off-limits to male searches."

Kevork clenched his fists in anger. "Sending Angele into a harem is not saving her," he said.

Nisa Hanim walked around her husband's desk and stood in front of Kevork. She towered over him with an unblinking gaze and said, "Set aside your prejudices."

Kevork stared back at her defiantly. "I am thankful for all that you and the doctor have done for the Armenians of Aleppo," he said. "But what you are suggesting now is not right."

Nisa Hanim sighed. "My cousin is an educated woman like me, and Angele will be as safe as anyone can be during a war."

Kevork did not respond for several minutes. He understood the risks Nisa Hanim had taken to set up this rescue plan for Angele. He looked across the desk. Dr. Aygun's face was tinged with exhaustion and ill health, but his look of determination matched his wife's.

Kevork took a deep breath and slowly exhaled. He forced his hands to unclench and felt the anger draining away from him. "What is the other choice?" he asked.

"This one is much more dangerous for Angele, but she would be helping the Armenian cause if she agrees to it," said Nisa Hanim.

She walked to a painting that was hanging on the wall and slid it sideways, revealing a small combination safe built into the wall. She turned the knob and the safe opened, revealing stacks of cash and a small unsealed envelope, its edges worn with much handling. She pulled the envelope out of the safe and set it on the desk in front of her husband. The doctor slid it over to Kevork.

Kevork opened the envelope. He could see the upper edges of two photographs. He slid them out, and then dropped them back on the desk as if he were holding a hot coal. The top one was a picture of dozens of children, starved to the bone, lying in the street. The children's eyes were half-closed and unseeing in death. What made the photo especially chilling was what it showed in one corner: a group of well-dressed Turks, stepping over the bodies as if doing so were a routine event.

Kevork had seen this scene a thousand times in real life, both when he was on the deportation march the year before and when he was delivering clandestine relief in the camps more recently. But to see it like this—recorded and permanent—was like a hand gripping his heart. He held the corner of the photograph between his thumb and index finger and reverently turned it over, and by doing so, he revealed the second photograph. This one was as troubling as the first. A mother, no more than a skeleton, lay on her back. Her arms were outstretched and in each arm was a dead child. Tears welled up in his throat as he stared at the mother and her children. He tried to comprehend the fact that a person with a camera had calmly snapped a shot while all around him, people were dying.

"They were dead already," whispered Nisa Hanim, her hand

gently brushing Kevork's forearm. "It was an American consul in Harput who took these."

Kevork looked up sharply. "Was it Leslie Davis?" he asked.

"Yes," she replied. "The man who was working with John Coren."

Kevork nodded in understanding. "How did you get them?" he asked.

"They were smuggled out," said the doctor. "By one of our couriers. There were many more, but the others were found and destroyed. These two photographs are our proof of mass murder."

Mass murder. Kevork had been focused on individual deaths—loved ones and people that he had met face to face. Even though he knew that the Turkish government was killing the Armenians, he hadn't really stopped to think about how the outside world would see it. If he hadn't seen thousands of dead and dying Armenians up close himself, would he have been able to believe it? And if he thought that way, what would people outside Turkey think when they heard about the mass killings? Who would believe it without proof?

Here was proof at his fingertips. Perhaps if he could get these photographs into the hands of foreigners, the world would begin to believe. Maybe Turkey could be forced to stop. He took a deep breath. Protecting the safety of these photographs was more important than his life.

"The Turkish government has been censoring the missionaries' mail for some time," continued Dr. Aygun. "Even here in Syria. I need your help to get these two photographs out."

"And how would I get them out?" asked Kevork.

"By carrying them," replied the doctor. "You could carry one and Angele could take the other."

"Surely there is a safer way to get this out?" asked Kevork.

"Perhaps a diplomat's pouch?" suggested Nisa Hanim with a sour look on her face.

"Yes," replied Kevork hopefully. "Wouldn't that work?"

"The government searches through those too," she said. "A priceless cache of photographs depicting the mass murders was recently apprehended from a diplomat's pouch. The photos were burned and the diplomat was killed."

Kevork felt a wave of exhaustion rise over him. It was over-whelming. Yes, he knew this was an important mission, and yes, he realized that he might die doing it. He was willing to take the risk. But what about Angele? Was it fair to expect a mere child to take the risk? His brotherly heart told him that if she traveled with him, he could protect her. His head told him that she would be safer with Nisa Hanim's cousin. He slumped down in his chair in resignation. "These photographs are more precious than my life," he said. "I will do what I can to take them safely out of the country."

"Thank you," said Nisa Hanim.

"But it is too dangerous for Angele."

Nisa Hanim sighed. "Of course, you are right," she said.

"Come with us," said Dr. Aygun. Kevork followed them to what appeared to be a storage room beside the office.

The doctor closed the door, and Kevork helped him push a wooden crate filled with medical supplies in front of it. He flipped back the threadbare Turkish carpet on the floor, revealing a trap door with a rope handle. Kevork crouched down and gave the handle a good tug. With a creak the door opened, and a faintly medicinal smell of disinfectant and soap wafted up. Kevork peered down and saw a rope ladder extending down to the dirt floor below.

Dr. Aygun went down first, followed by Nisa Hanim and then Kevork. The basement was so low that Kevork's head nearly touched the ceiling. Stacks of medical supplies in crates lined the stone walls. Zeki sat at a small, scrubbed table with a *dama* (Turkish checkers) board in front of him, his chin cupped in one hand and a look of concentration on his face. There was a plate with remnants of lunch and two empty mugs beside the dama board. The smoking stub of a candle nestled in a saucer in the middle of the table, and there were several cushions on the floor. Dr. Aygun lit the candle.

At first, Kevork couldn't see Angele, but as his eyes got used to the dim light, Angele appeared in the shadows beside a stack of crates. Her hair was recently washed and it was braided down her back. Her eyes looked huge with fear. She wore an old pair of Zeki's cast-off trousers and a threadbare shirt.

"It is safe," said Dr. Aygun in a comforting whisper to Angele. She looked from the doctor to Kevork, and then her face lit up with recognition. She leapt into Kevork's arms. He hugged her tightly. She smelled faintly of lice soap. "You are safe," he said. "Thank God."

"I knew you would find me," said Angele.

The warmth of Angele safe in his arms banished his exhaustion. He thought of all the loved ones he had lost: his sister killed before his eyes, his father dead and mother missing. Dear Aunt Anna, killed while saving Marta's life. What of Onnig and Mariam? Were they still alive? And Marta...?

All that Kevork knew was that Angele was still alive. He never wanted to let her out of his sight again, but he knew that wouldn't be fair to her. She would be safer with Nisa Hanim's cousin.

"Perhaps we should ask Angele herself what she wants to do with her life?" asked Dr. Aygun. His wife nodded.

Kevork set Angele back down on the dirt floor.

"What do you mean?" asked Angele. The doctor explained.

She looked from the doctor's face to Kevork's face in panic. "You won't leave me, will you?" she asked him.

"It would be safer if you stayed with Nisa Hanim's cousin," said Kevork.

"I won't!" she said. She wrapped her arms around Kevork's waist, resting her head on his chest. "I have no family left," she said, "but you are the brother I never had. I would rather die with you than live without you."

Kevork held Angele close to him and rocked her back and forth. He was overcome with emotion. "And you are my little sister," he said.

The doctor spoke. "It is decided. Angele will accompany you. Let us go upstairs and prepare you both for your journey."

Kevork bent his head in resignation, and Angele grinned with joy.

When they climbed up the ladder, Zeki dashed ahead as Dr. Aygun led them through a back door and into the family's living quarters. They walked through a room where richly detailed carpets covered the floor and hung on the walls, and a low, enameled table was surrounded by embroidered cushions. Kevork and Angele followed the doctor and his wife into a back room that seemed to be a combination storage area and cooking space. Zeki stood at the far end of a long wooden table and set out various food items—small cucumbers, cheese, olives, tomatoes, and dried fruit.

Dr. Aygun watched his son's preparations with pride and nodded in approval. Kevork felt a flash of jealousy. His own parents had disappeared when he was Zeki's age, and his memories of them were dimming as each day passed. Watching the silent understanding between father and son made Kevork realize with a sharp pang everything he had lost. He tried to push the thoughts out of his head. The Ayguns were singularly good people. Kevork's gaze rested on Dr. Aygun's tightened belt, and he regarded the man's sallow complexion. How long did he have to live? This family deserved any happiness they could scrape out of life.

"Where are they going?" asked Zeki as he placed several enamel mugs on the table.

"To Smyrna," replied his mother. "And they need to leave tonight."

"You want us to go back into Turkey?" asked Kevork with surprise. "Surely we will be caught."

"You may be," said Nisa Hanim. "But Smyrna is on the coast and is mostly Greek. It is not a likely place to be looking for Armenians."

She opened up a heavy wooden box that was pushed against one of the walls and knelt in front of it. She drew out a pair of walking boots.

"Come here, dear," said Nisa Hanim to Angele. "These belonged to Zeki when he was younger. See if you can get your feet into them."

Angele took the boots and stared at them in awe. She held them to her nose and breathed in the scent of leather. "They're beautiful," she said. "Are you sure you don't need them for someone else?"

"They're yours if they fit," said Nisa Hanim kindly, taking one of the boots back from Angele and loosening the laces.

Angele slipped her foot into the boot. "It is plenty big enough," she said with a look of wonder in her eyes. Kevork suspected that she had never worn boots or shoes before.

Then Nisa Hanim pulled out a bright blue tunic. She held it up to Angele's shoulders and frowned. "Maybe too big," she murmured to herself. She dug around in the chest and found a smaller tunic in pale green. She held it up. "Perfect," she said. "And here's a pair of trousers that should fit."

Angele wrapped her arms around the bundle of clothing, blinking in confusion. "Do you want me to change into these?"

"Yes, dear," said Nisa Hanim. "Go into the other room so you have some privacy."

While Angele changed, the doctor wrapped one of the photographs in a silk cloth.

When Angele returned, Kevork regarded her with surprise. She was dressed in the kind of outfit that most Turkish females wore indoors, away from prying eyes.

He turned to Nisa Hanim. "How is she supposed to travel in that outfit?"

"Hidden under a chador," said Nisa Hanim. "That will hide her scarred hands. It will also hide the fact that she is very young."

Kevork frowned in confusion. "A veiled girl traveling with a single man? Surely we will attract attention."

"On the contrary," said Nisa Hanim, a faint smile forming on her lips. "You will be traveling as a married couple."

"But she is tiny," protested Kevork. "People will know she is just a child."

"There are child brides in this country," said Nisa Hanim.

Kevork blinked in surprise. Yes, of course. But the thought of little Angele as someone's wife made the bile rise in his throat. She had not yet had a childhood. He looked over at Angele and she grinned at him. Perhaps to her it was an innocent game. He had to acknowledge that the chador would be an ideal hiding place for one of the photos.

"Please pass me your rucksack," said the doctor to Kevork.

"Certainly," said Kevork, surprised. He picked it up from the floor and handed it to Dr. Aygun.

The doctor turned it upside down and dumped the contents onto the table. Kevork's prayer rug and the remnant of Angele's sunburst carpet tumbled out.

Angele's eyes lit up with joy at the sight of it. "You saved my carpet!" Kevork handed it to her and she held it to her chest. "Thank you," she said.

Kevork's shoemaking tools also tumbled out onto the table. "You may need these on your journey," said the doctor. He picked up the needles and thread, the pieces of leather, the awl and knife, and two tin cups made out of cans. It was all he possessed in the whole world. Even if they wouldn't come in handy, he didn't want to give them up.

The doctor turned the rucksack inside out, examining its construction carefully. "If we open up these stitches here," he said, brushing the tip of his finger along the bottom of the sack, "we should be able to slip the photograph inside."

"Am I to carry a rucksack too?" asked Angele.

"It would be unseemly," said Nisa Hanim. "Kevork will have to carry everything in order to keep up appearances."

With a small pair of scissors, Dr. Aygun carefully ripped out the stitches along the one interior edge of Kevork's rucksack, then he slid the silk covered photograph in place. He held the edges together as Kevork carefully stitched it shut with his needle and thread. When the job was done, he turned the rucksack right side out again. The photograph was perfectly hidden. Kevork repacked his tools, his prayer mat, and Angele's carpet. Nisa Hanim gave him a cloth package filled with dried fruit and bread for their journey. He put that in his rucksack and slung it over his shoulder.

Nisa Hanim went back to the wooden chest and drew out a long apricot-colored silk scarf. She folded the second photograph into a sheer silk cloth, then folded the scarf around it. "Wear this around your waist under the chador like this," said the doctor's wife, wrapping the scarf around Angele's waist so that the photo was snug against the small of her back.

Dr. Aygun, who had been quiet through this exchange, reached into his breast pocket and pulled out a stack of bills, a large manila envelope, and a folded sheet of paper. "These will assist in your travels," he said.

Kevork tucked the cash into the folds of his robe, and then he unfolded the piece of paper and scanned the contents. "I am in the employ of the Germans?" he asked, raising his eyebrows in surprise.

"Your guise is that of a courier for a German businessman in Smyrna," said the doctor. "You are to deliver that envelope to him."

"And is that where we are truly going?" asked Kevork.

"Yes," replied Dr. Aygun. "Herr Bloch of the Baghdad Railway Company is stationed at Smyrna. He is sympathetic to the Armenian cause. His interpreter is an Armenian named Sarkis Gregorian, and it is to him you will deliver the photographs."

"And then?" asked Kevork.

"Gregorian will get the photos into American hands," replied the doctor.

Kevork nodded in understanding.

"As for you and Angele, Smyrna is mostly Greek, and it is far from the main deportation routes," said Dr. Aygun. "You should be safe there until the war ends."

"Thank you for all that you've done," said Kevork. "May you stay safe."

The doctor and his wife bowed solemnly, and Angele and Kevork returned the gesture. Zeki held out his hand to Angele. Instead of taking it, she wrapped her arms around his shoulders and gave him a kiss on the cheek. "Thank you, Zeki," she said.

"You are a true friend." Zeki's cheeks turned a bright pink and he stammered a good-bye.

Nisa Hanim showed Angele how to wear the chador. "It is dark now," she said, wrapping it into a tidy bundle and tucking it into Kevork's rucksack. "But before the call to prayer at sunrise, be sure to cover yourself up with it."

The young girl solemnly nodded. Kevork took Angele's hand and led her up the stairs and onto the roof. "That's where we're heading," he said, pointing to the neighboring roof that was separated from the Ayguns' by a three-foot gap. "On the count of three, we jump."

Eighteen

KEVORK

Kevork and Angele traveled from rooftop to rooftop until the railway station was in sight. There was a tumbledown shack not too far from the station, so they decided to rest there for the night. The collapsed roof curved around them like a cradle and they fell into an uneasy sleep. When the first rays of morning sunlight hit Kevork's eyes, he sat up. In the middle of the night he had taken the chador out of his rucksack and wrapped it around Angele like a blanket.

He shook her arm gently and she opened her eyes. He smoothed the wrinkles out of the chador and helped her get into it.

"Your name will be Melek," he said. "It means 'angel' in Turkish."

Angele smiled.

"One more thing before we go," he said. He worked the wedding ring off his baby finger and placed it into Angele's palm.

She picked it up between her thumb and index finger with her other hand and held it up to her eyes. "Why are you giving this to me?" she asked. Then she looked into Kevork's eyes. "This is for Marta."

"You are supposed to be my wife right now," said Kevork. "It would look strange for me to be wearing a woman's wedding band on my baby finger, while your ring finger is bare."

138

Angele clasped the wedding ring in her hand, then held it to her heart. "I will wear this for Marta," she said. Then she slipped it onto her ring finger.

Kevork threw his rucksack to the ground. He jumped down beside it, then reached up and helped Angele down, being careful not to catch her chador on the rusted edge of the roof. He slung the rucksack over his back and walked toward the train station. Angele kept a few steps behind him, mimicking the way she had seen Turkish wives walk behind their men.

There were soldiers milling around the train station, as well as a couple of Arab men. One had a goat with a rope around its neck. There was also a heavyset woman in a chador accompanied by a Turkish man. Kevork was comforted by the sight of the woman. Perhaps he and Angele would blend in after all.

A lineup had formed in front of the ticket booth, so Kevork and Angele joined the end of the line. When they got up to the front, Kevork drew a few bills from the folds of his robe and placed them on the counter. "Two tickets to Bozanti, please."

The ticket agent looked up from behind his spectacles and gave Kevork a once-over, taking in the distinctive blue tattoos on Kevork's temples and his Arab dress. Then he looked beyond Kevork and regarded the tiny figure shrouded in a chador. The man smirked knowingly and winked. He handed Kevork two tickets. Kevork took them, his face flushing in humiliation. What kind of man must he think I am? he thought in disgust.

He turned from the ticket booth and walked briskly to the dusty, open-air waiting area, Angele close at his heels. They had waited with the others in the hot sun for an hour or more, when in the distance they could hear a train arriving from the southwest. As it shuddered to a halt, Kevork saw that there were several boxcars, with soldiers riding on the outside ledges of each one.

The soldiers from the first boxcar jumped down and opened up the wide sliding doors. Kevork was nearly knocked to the ground by the overpowering stench of death and disease. The boxcar was stacked six deep with bodies, mostly women and children and a few old men. The soldiers prodded the bodies with their bayonets. Some of the corpses fell to the ground, but others were not yet dead, and the sharp points of the bayonets brought them back to life. Kevork watched in horror as a naked woman—so thin that every rib stood out in sharp relief—hobbled off the train. She reached back in and helped others who still lived out of the boxcar. A moment later, the second boxcar opened, and then the next and the next.

Kevork could hear Angele try to restrain her sobs as she stood beside him. He was thankful that the chador covered her emotions; he had no such advantage and had to swallow back his sorrow so that no one would suspect his sympathy.

One of the soldiers stepped forward. "This way," he said, prodding the naked woman from the first boxcar and the few others who were still able to walk. Kevork watched as the deportees shambled away, encircled by soldiers. They would be taken to one of the many concentration camps just outside the city gates. It was unlikely that any of them would live much longer.

A short time later, another train entered the station, this time from the northeast. Unlike the first, it was not filled with deportees. The train consisted of mostly empty boxcars and a single passenger car. Kevork and Angele lined up with the others. There were still some soldiers leaning against the station wall, smoking cigarettes and talking amongst themselves. But none of them got in line.

Once their tickets were punched and Kevork and Angele were allowed onto the train, the conductor led them to a set of seats facing each other. There was a window overlooking the train station on one side, and a set of lockable sliding doors on the other.

Angele sat by the window, arranging her chador to ensure that she was completely covered. Kevork sat beside her. Angele began to speak, but Kevork held his index finger to his lips. "Silence for now," he said quietly.

They sat for ten minutes. Fifteen minutes. Thirty minutes passed and the train had not moved. Neither said a word. The lockable doors remained open. Once, a soldier passed, poked his head in, and then moved along. Another time, the Arab with the goat walked by, ignoring them completely. Then the conductor came and rechecked their tickets.

An hour passed, and the train was still sitting idle in the station. Two soldiers with rifles boarded the train. He could hear them go from compartment to compartment, checking the occupants.

There was a faint scent of tobacco and sweat as the two soldiers loomed in the doorway of Kevork and Angele's compartment.

"Names?" said one of the soldiers in a bored voice.

"Khedive Ayakkabici," said Kevork with polite reserve.

"And the woman?"

"My wife, Melek." Kevork replied. He held his breath.

The soldiers nodded disinterestedly and walked away.

Relieved, Kevork slumped in his seat.

Thirty minutes later, the train finally began to pull out of the station. Kevork slid the doors shut and locked them.

"Where will we go once we reach Smyrna?" asked Angele in a low whisper.

"First we have to get there," replied Kevork.

⤚ ⤙

Kevork stared out the window as the train slowly sped past the buildings of Aleppo and beyond the city gates. When the view

141

changed to a vast expanse of dry, rocky hills, Kevork gave in to the rhythmic chugging of the train and felt some of his pent-up anxiety diminish. But every time they stopped, his anxiety returned.

At every stop were encampments of ragged Armenian deportees, some with enormous wicker baskets filled with their worldly belongings. Others had nothing more than the clothing on their backs. The least fortunate didn't even have that anymore. Many had pitched tents made of flimsy cloth and they seemed to be going nowhere. There were soldiers at the stops too, but it was unclear what their plans were for the deportees. Were they helping the deportees to be shipped out or marched southeast into the desert like so many Armenians before them? Or were they waiting for the uprooted deportees to die where they were? Kevork watched as village men lined up to get on and off the train, and he marveled at their ability to be blind to the presence of the misery that surrounded them.

Kevork kept the sliding doors closed and locked most of the time, but at one long stop, a man got on the train to sell flat bread and meat on a skewer. Kevork bought enough food and water for both of them. At first Angele shook her head. "I am not feeling well," she said.

"I don't feel like eating either," he said, looking out at the deportees just a stone's throw away. When was the last time they had eaten? he wondered. "But we must keep up our strength."

Angele lifted the chador and extended her hand. "Perhaps a bit of water then," she said in a shaky voice.

Kevork gave her water, cautioning her to sip it frugally; there was no lavatory on the train. "And eat this," he said, breaking off a piece of the flat bread and placing it in her hand. She took it, but hours later, Kevork noticed that she hadn't eaten a single bite.

It took the whole day to reach the end of the rail line at

Islohia. The train stopped at dusk. "We need to get off the train here and get onto the one continuing to Bozanti in the morning," explained Kevork as he unlocked the doors to their compartment, then slid them open.

He slung his rucksack over one shoulder, then paused at the entrance to their compartment as people walked past them to get off the train. Angele stood up and clutched Kevork's elbow. He turned and tried to see her face through the chador. "Are you feeling unwell?" he asked.

"A bit of a headache is all," she answered. "Once I get some fresh air, I should be fine." She waited beside him until the last person had left, and then they stepped into the aisle together and walked toward the exit.

Kevork had thought that he was immune to all horrors at this point, but nothing could have prepared him for the sight at Islohia. The first thing that greeted them when they stepped off the train was an overpowering stench. It was one that Kevork was all too familiar with: decomposing corpses. He turned his head and saw a huge mound of dead bodies right beside the platform. A rubbish pile of dead Armenians who had been left there to rot.

Angele gripped Kevork's elbow as they passed. He felt her stumble and sob. "Keep moving, Melek Hanim," he whispered, wrapping his arm about her waist and pulling her away from the mound of corpses. Kevork covered his mouth with his hand and suppressed a gag. On the top were the bodies of women who looked almost alive: naked and with long hair tangled and matted. At the bottom of the pile amidst the bones he could make out a tiny skull with a bit of flesh and hair still clinging to it, and the delicate joints of a baby's skeletonized hand—the rest of the baby's remains had been crushed by the weight of the many victims on top of it. How long had this pile been accumulating?

Were the townspeople so used to the sight of dying Armenians that this pile was unremarkable? Kevork could only imagine.

Angele gasped aloud in sorrow. He gripped her tightly and steered her off the platform. He hoped the chador had protected her from the most gruesome details.

A man in a long Arabic robe like Kevork's own stood by, smoking a cigarette. He was leaning against the side of a building that was farthest away from the mound of corpses. As Angele and Kevork passed, he said in Arabic, "Do you need a place to stay for the night?"

"Yes," answered Kevork.

"Follow me."

As they followed the man through the dusty streets and into the oldest part of the village, they passed clusters of deportees crouching at the sides of the road, holding out their hands for a bit of bread. The man did not seem to notice them. Kevork and Angele could not stop and help them. Even if they could, what could they give them? The food and cash they carried was enough to get them to Smyrna and for bribes if necessary. They had to get those photos out. Kevork tried to swallow back his overwhelming despair. Any help that came from the outside world would be too late to help these people on the street. And even if he and Angele were able to smuggle the photographs out, how many days, weeks, and months would pass before the world intervened? It all seemed hopeless. Kevork felt utterly useless.

As they walked through the streets, vendors gathered to sell their wares, taking advantage of the train's new arrivals. Kevork had not set foot in Turkey since being marched out at the point of a bayonet a year earlier. As he looked at the friendly townspeople offering their wares, or simply walking past without a second look, he remembered how the townspeople had lined the road to spit

and jeer at him and the other Armenians rounded up to march out
into the desert. What would these people do now if they found
out that he and Angele were Armenians?

The room was simple, with a single deep-set window high up
on an angled wall and a wooden chest directly below. There was a
wash basin with a jug of water on top of the chest and a small
woven carpet on the floor.

The two beds were narrow with thin, lumpy mattresses and bedding that didn't look exactly clean. Kevork strung a blanket across
the room, tying one end to a hook and the other to a wooden post.

"There," he said, smiling at Angele. "You have some privacy."

Angele shook her head. "I'm cold," she said. "Can you hold me?"

That night, he lay on one of the lumpy mattresses, with Angele
nestled in his arms and the blankets wrapped around her. She shivered through the night. He listened to her troubled breathing. The
air at Islohia, fetid with corpses, had entered her lungs. He held her
tight, but she didn't fall asleep until the early hours of the morning. He was glad that she was finally able to sleep. She had been
through so much. His arm was numb from holding her, so he
turned onto his other side, trying to find a comfortable position. It
was impossible to sleep; images of deportees kept tumbling
through his mind. But it was more than that. The next stop along
their route was Adana, the region of his birth. He hadn't been there
since the 1909 massacres. What would it be like now?

～†～

The next day on the train, a soldier sat across from them. Kevork
wondered if he was sitting in their compartment because the
train was otherwise full, or to keep an eye on them. Whatever the
reason, the result was the same: he and Angele remained jittery
and silent.

145

The train stopped for half a day not far from Kevork's old village in Adana. Kevork had hoped that the train would go quickly through his old village, but he had forgotten about the fork in the train tracks. The soldier across from them settled in for a long nap.

"Let us get some air, Melek Hanim," he said to Angele. They left the sleeping soldier to himself and stepped out of the compartment. Kevork helped Angele down the steps and together they walked toward the village of his birth. In the distance was the distinctive stone bridge that spanned across the Jihan River. As they stepped through the stone gates of the little village, Kevork saw the familiar haphazard row of clay one-story homes. Each home still had a flat roof that doubled as a terrace, and each still had a walled-in fruit and vegetable garden where a goat or a few chickens could run free. It was as if time had stood still. With Angele a few steps behind him, Kevork weaved through the twisting alleyway until it opened up to a wide square, where there was a communal well. There used to be an Armenian church here, but it had been transformed into a cow barn. And at the well, instead of Armenian women with veils covering their hair but not their faces, there were Turkish women, completely covered in black chadors. Two Turkish men sat on either side of a dama board, and several other men stood close by, watching the game and smoking cigarettes.

"This was the Armenian district," Kevork whispered to Angele. Then he led her to what used to be his own house. There were two young Turkish boys in the courtyard, trying to climb up the fig tree. The younger stood barefoot on the shoulders of his older brother, who boosted him up onto a sturdy branch. Kevork's heart lurched at the sight. How many times had he and his friends done the same thing so many years ago? Bile rose in his throat.

It was as if Armenians had been erased from the history and the memory of his birth town.

"Let's go back to the train," he said to Angele.

When they reached their compartment, the soldier had just woken up. He shifted in his seat to let them sit down and followed Kevork's gaze out of the window. He looked back at Kevork. "It has been successfully Turkified," said the soldier.

"Allah is good," replied Kevork with a nod. He hoped he looked sincere.

As they pulled out of Adana, the clouds broke and the Tarsus Mountains came into view. Angele craned her neck to see. "They are beautiful," she said.

Kevork nodded. Anything was better than corpses, he thought. Or memories.

The train chugged through the mountains for the rest of the day and Kevork began to relax. He even fell asleep for a few hours, as did Angele, her head nestled in the crook of his arm. The soldier was gone when he woke. Kevork's arm was wet with sweat so he extricated himself from Angele, who was still sound asleep. He set his rucksack down on the seat as a pillow for her and then tucked her chador around her. He sat on the opposite seat and looked out of the window. It was still mountains and blue horizon. No more deportees. They had traveled beyond the deportation route.

Angele groaned, then pushed herself to a half-sitting position. She was shivering violently.

Kevork got up from his seat and knelt down beside her. He lifted the black veil of her chador and felt her forehead. It was clammy and hot. "Do you have a headache?" he asked.

She nodded.

"And sore muscles?"

"Yes," she whispered hoarsely.

Typhus. How could it be? It was so unfair. He had finally got Angele away from the deportation areas. Kevork wrapped his arms around Angele and drew her to his chest. His body heat warmed her a bit, but she kept on shivering. At last she fell back into an uneasy sleep.

Hours later, the train halted at Bozanti. The tracks had not been completed beyond this point. Angele was too weak to walk, so Kevork slung his rucksack over one shoulder and gathered Angele in his arms and carried her off the train.

He approached a man who was standing on the train platform holding a sign that read, Room for Rent.

"Is the room far from here?" asked Kevork.

The man looked at Angele and shook his head. "She's sick," he said. "I don't want no sickness in my rooms."

"Is there a hospital in this town?" asked Kevork.

"There is," said the man. "But it's full of sick people." He spat on the ground. "Best place to take her is somewhere with no other people."

The man pointed Kevork in the direction of a *khan* at the out-skirts of town. Kevork's arms ached with Angele's weight by the time he reached the rest house. The owner was not much con-cerned with Angele's ailment. "Make yourself comfortable," he said, pushing open the door to his barn as he pocketed Kevork's coins. The stables reeked of horse manure, and the hay was mov-ing with vermin. Still holding Angele in his arms, he bowed to the man, thanking him for his hospitality. Once the man was out of sight, Kevork carried Angele up the ladder and to the roof of the khan. It smelled better on the roof, but the evening breeze sent Angele into another spasm of shivers.

"Hold me tight," she said. He spent the night holding her, and giving her bits of water when she could swallow it. By morning, her face and arms were covered in livid sores. Just as Sister Helena had done for him, he tried to keep Angele warm when she shivered and cool when she was covered in sweat. He bathed her forehead with water and forced her to drink tiny sips of water. He nurtured her for nearly a week, but she wasn't strong enough to fight off the typhus.

She died in his arms one Sunday at sunrise.

As the muezzins chanted the morning prayer, Kevork drew the wedding ring off her cold finger and put it back on his own. Then he held her and wept. She had been a constant in his life since he had come to Aleppo and the thought of never hearing her voice or her laughter again drove him mad with despair. It was like losing his sister all over again.

He carried her body to the local graveyard, but it stank of too much death, so he carried her out of Bozanti. He found a secluded spot in a green valley nestled between the mountains and buried her there. But before he did, he unwrapped the silk apricot scarf from around her waist and carefully tied it beneath his own robe, making sure that the photograph was snug against the small of his back.

He said a prayer for his angel as he placed the last handful of dirt on her grave. Then he lay down beside the grave and wept. It was his fault that she had died. He should have insisted that she stay with Nisa Hanim's sister. He wept until no more tears would come and then he fell into a guilty sleep.

Untold hours later, he awoke. It took him a few moments to remember where he was. He began to weep anew, but then he stopped. The photographs were more important than his life or Angele's. He stood up, brushing the dirt from his hands. He was dead tired and emotionally devastated. But he had to get the photographs smuggled out.

And he had to find Marta.

He slung his rucksack over his shoulder and turned west. Toward Smyrna. And he began to walk.

Nineteen

ZEKI

Zeki wrapped the new wad of cash from John Coren into a piece of cloth and shoved it down the front of his shirt. It wasn't a good hiding place and he knew it, but this was an emergency. With Kevork gone, there were no dependable couriers left, and Miss Amelia needed this money. Besides, he reasoned, who would stop a little boy? He tiptoed out the front entrance of the house after everyone was asleep, making sure to quietly lock the door and slip the key into his trouser pocket before stepping away from the house.

The streets were empty, save for the beggars who were curled up asleep alongside the buildings and one wild dog who snarled at him as he passed. Once, he thought he heard footsteps behind him, but when he turned there was no one there. It didn't take him long to get to the old wooden house with ornately carved shutters at the edge of town. He pulled the rope on the bell at the gate and waited.

No answer.

He knocked on the door, quietly at first, and when no one answered, he knocked so hard that his knuckles smarted. Still no answer. He picked up a stone from the ground and climbed halfway up the gate. He threw the stone at the window but missed.

Why wasn't Miss Amelia coming to the door? She was expecting him, after all. In frustration, he pulled on the gate door with all his might and almost lost his balance when it flew open.

He stepped through the gate and walked into the courtyard. It looked silvered and menacing in the moonlight with the branches of bare trees reaching out at him like skeletal hands. He walked briskly up the steps and to the door and tried the handle. Like the gate, it was unlocked. He stepped in. Silence. He walked down the hallway. Miss Amelia's office door was ajar so he looked inside. She wasn't there. Papers were scattered across her desk and onto the floor.

He backed out of the office and headed to the end of the hallway. He knew that the boys slept in the room on the right and the girls slept in the room to the left. He pushed the boys' door open.

No children were sleeping. Bedclothes were tumbled and torn. And there was a bloody footprint of a soldier's boot at the base of one of the beds.

Had they all been sent to Deir Ez Zor? What about Miss Amelia? He had to get back and tell his parents. He ran down the hallway and out the front door. Then he stopped. A silhouette in the moonlight. It was the soldier with the brown leather strap.

In the half-darkness, Zeki watched as the soldier lifted his rifle and aimed.

"No!" cried Zeki, holding his arms to his chest.

Then he felt a thwack on his forearm and a thump in his chest. The force of the bullets knocked him to the ground. The last thing Zeki felt as he died was the soldier rooting through his clothing. The soldier found the money. And the key.

"Off to visit your parents now," said the soldier with a chuckle.

151

John Coren pushed himself farther into the shadows along the wall of the courtyard, hoping the soldier wouldn't see him. He had to cover his mouth tightly with both hands so that he wouldn't gasp or cry out. He stayed like that for moments—horror-stricken in the dark. After he was sure that the soldier was truly gone, he ran to Zeki's body and put his fingers on his neck, feeling for a pulse. There was none.

John looked up at the moon through the branches. "Why, God?" he cried. "Why did you take this little boy?" Then he gathered Zeki's still-warm body into his arms and carried him into the house. He gently set the body down on a cot in the boys' dormitory and covered it up with a sheet. If the authorities came back, they would assume that this was just one more dead Armenian. John wished he could do more for Zeki—at least give him a proper burial—but there were more urgent things that he had to do.

Running would have called attention to his actions, so instead he walked swiftly down the street in a manner that would look leisurely to the casual observer. It drove him wild not to run, but he had no choice. By the time he got to the Aygun house, he knew he was too late. The soldier was just coming out of the door with a look of satisfaction on his face. In the moonlight, John Coren saw that the bayonet on the soldier's rifle was streaked with blood. With calm deliberation, the soldier took the key from his pocket and relocked the door.

John groaned in despair. Had the soldier left the door open, he would have been able to find the Ayguns quickly. They might be still alive. Just then John remembered the roof entry to the house—the one that Zeki always used. In the moonlight, John used the window ledge to hoist himself onto the roof. As he stood, his eyes darting around in the darkness for the entrance, he felt a fluttering against his cheek. His heart skipped a beat. But then he felt the fluttering again and the slight pressure of bird's claws on his shoulder. It was Zeki's rock dove, Jujij.

"Who will look after you, now, little bird?" he asked, his grief renewed. John had no crumbs to give him. The bird flew off, as if knowing that sustenance would no longer be found there. John whispered a prayer. And then he found the entrance.

As he stepped down into the quiet house, his nose wrinkled at the distinctive metallic smell of fresh blood. He followed the scent to where it was the strongest and came upon an open door—the Ayguns' bedroom. There, in the moonlight, he could see Dr. Aygun, lying on his back, his mouth half open in death. His throat had been slashed so deeply that his neck was nearly severed. His wife, Nisa Hanim, lay on her side, her head nestled in the crook of her husband's arm and her knees tucked under his legs. The front of her nightgown was covered with blood. It looked as if she had been stabbed first, then tried to cover her husband's body with her own to protect him.

John said a brief prayer and covered them with a sheet.

He walked back down the corridor and found Nisa Hanim's office. The door was ajar and papers were scattered about, but John was relieved to see that the picture was in its place. The soldier did not know about the safe. John opened it and quickly looked through the contents: contact information for Kevork in Smyrna; a bundle of money; a listing of the underground couriers and what mission they were currently on. Thank God these records had not been found. John stuffed the cash into his coat and held on to the list. He walked back to the desk and looked at the papers scattered about.

A telegram from Smyrna sat in full view. It was from the American merchant who had agreed to get the photos out once the courier brought them there. This, John knew, was a death sentence. The American merchant would be found and would meet with an accident.

Who could be trusted to get the photos to America? There was only one person—himself. And if he was killed in the attempt, it was a price John was willing to pay.

He took a match out of his pocket and lit it, then set fire to the papers on the desk. He stood there for a moment to make sure that the fire had taken, and then he left the Aygun house through the rooftop exit.

~~~†~~~

With the stack of money from the Ayguns' safe, John bought himself a car, a flashy new suit, and a case of whiskey. Then he set out on the road to Smyrna. He had only traveled a mile or two out of Aleppo when his car was stopped for the first time.

"Out," said the soldier, looking John up and down with disgust.

John got out of the car, holding an opened bottle of whiskey in his hand. "What is the problem?" he asked the soldier in a slurred voice.

"There is a war on," said the soldier, "in case you hadn't noticed."

"I do know," said John. "And that's why I'm leaving." He took a swig of whiskey from the bottle, then offered it to the soldier. "Thirsty?" he asked.

The soldier shook his head in disapproval. "You Americans," he said. "You think this is all a big joke."

John grinned maniacally. "Not at all, not at all, my friend," he said. "I want to get out of this as fast as I can."

"We just have to search you and your car, and you can be on your way," said the soldier.

The soldier had John strip down to his underwear. Every seam of his suit, shirt, tie, and shoes were examined minutely. Two other soldiers went through every inch of his car with the same thoroughness.

"You're fine," said the soldier. "Get on your way, and good riddance."

John was stopped over and over again on the first week or so of his trip, but after that, the searches stopped. He could only assume that the soldiers had wired ahead to inform them that a harmless, drunken American buffoon was heading their way.

Twenty

MARIAM AND MARTA

Mariam opened the door wide and let Mr. Brighton step in. "But where can we hide?" she asked. "They will be searching everywhere."

Mr. Brighton regarded Marta and the baby. Mariam could see the panic in his eyes.

"I don't know," he said. "But this is the first place they will look."

Marta lifted her head. "I have an idea," she said. "Ask Nurse Bowley to meet us in the laundry."

Mr. Brighton nodded and rushed out the door.

"What is your idea?" asked Mariam.

"No time to explain," said Marta. She turned to Sheruk-rey-ah. "Go to the girls' dorm," she said. "You must look and act like one of them."

Sheruk-rey-ah's face paled at the suggestion, but she nodded in agreement. She had avoided the other children since her arrival.

"Go. Now!" said Marta. Sheruk-rey-ah bolted out the door.

Marta turned; her sister was hastily getting dressed. "No time for that," said Marta. "We must get out of here."

With the baby still at her breast, Marta shrugged off the blanket and stood up. She walked quickly to the door. With her free hand, she pushed it open.

Mariam held the stinking swaddling clothes in front of her with both hands as she trotted alongside her sister. She frowned in confusion. "Where are we going to hide?" she asked.

"I am still trying to figure that out," said Marta. "But I think I have an idea."

Sheruk-rey-ah ran barefoot to the children's dormitory, still dressed in the wrinkled Turkish tunic and trousers that she had been wearing since her arrival. Despite the early hour, a cluster of urchins were playing a stone-toss game outside the door. Sheruk-rey-ah blanched when she saw that one of the boys was Hrag—the boy who had thrown a stone at her and called her names the day before.

"There's the little Turkish whore," called Hrag to the others as Sheruk-rey-ah approached the dormitory door. One of the younger boys ran to the door and blocked her way.

"The dormitory's not for Turks," said the boy. "Go away."

"You don't understand!" said Sheruk-rey-ah urgently. "Soldiers are coming. They're inspecting us all."

Hrag blinked in astonishment at this news. "Let her through," he said to the younger boy. "And go wake everyone up to let them know."

Sheruk-rey-ah barreled through the door. She ran down the corridor to the left, which opened onto the area where the girls slept. Hrag and the others turned right. In the old days, this whole dormitory would have been filled with girls, and the boys would have been on the other side of the complex, at Beitshalom Orphanage for Boys. But there were so few adults and so few children, that everyone was clustered into a few buildings.

"Awake, awake!" shouted Sheruk-rey-ah as she entered the girls' sleeping area. "The soldiers are coming!"

The girls bolted out of their beds and quickly tidied themselves and their beds, rolling their bedrolls into neat bundles. One of the older girls named Nadalia looked at Sheruk-rey-ah with concern. "Get out of that clothing," she said. "The soldiers will know that you have just arrived, and then the questions will really start."

Nadalia pulled roughly at Sheruk-rey-ah's tunic and had it over her head and stuffed inside a bedroll in a flash. "Here," she said, handing Sheruk-rey-ah a coarse tunic. "Put it on."

Another girl pulled a bedroll out of the cupboard. "Put this on the last bed," she said to Sheruk-rey-ah. "It has to look like you have been here awhile."

Sheruk-rey-ah was overwhelmed by the girls' immediate acceptance of her. She had expected them to shun her. "What is your name?" Nadalia asked.

"Parantzim," said Sheruk-rey-ah.

When Mariam and Marta got to the laundry, Sarah Baji was there, as Marta knew she would be, soaking the bloodied sheets and clothing from Pauline's birth in the great vat filled with cold water.

Marta turned to her sister. "Get buckets and fill the laundry tub closer to the brim," she said.

"But why?" asked Mariam.

"That is where we will be hiding," replied Marta.

"But all this blood. What will they think?"

Marta didn't answer her sister. Instead, she turned to Sarah Baji. "I want you to throw some of the clean laundry into the tub, just to give it bulk. But make sure that the bloodied laundry is on the top."

Sarah Baji nodded and got to work.

Just then, the door opened and Nurse Bowley walked in, her mop of light brown hair matted with sleep on one side, and her white blouse haphazardly buttoned. Marta explained her plan. Nurse Bowley's eyebrows raised in surprise. "Yes. It could work," she said.

While Mariam filled the giant tub with buckets of water and Sarah Baji arranged the clean clothing underneath the bloodied linens, Marta sat calmly, nursing Pauline. She forced herself to breathe slowly, evenly. Pauline had to be calm. Pauline could not cry.

"Where are we going to put the baby?" Mariam asked her sister as she dumped in a final bucket of water into the laundry tub.

"I don't know," said Marta, forcing her voice to remain calm.

"This is a good place," said Sarah Baji. She pointed to a wicker basket filled with fresh laundry that was waiting to be sorted and folded. "We will put the baby in the middle, underneath some folded linens. If she stays quiet, she'll be completely hidden."

Marta knew it wasn't a perfect solution, but it was the best they had. Just then, Marta heard Mr. Brighton speaking in a loud voice outside. He was answering a soldier's question. "The time is now!" she said.

Sarah Baji gently took Pauline from Marta's arms, then Marta tried to hoist herself up to the side of the tub, but she was too weak. Mariam quickly lifted her sister and dropped her in with a splash. "Ooohhh, it is so cold!" whispered Marta. She filled her lungs with air and then dunked her head under the dirty laundry.

Mariam hoisted herself up to the edge, and with her remaining strength managed to get both legs over the side and into the tub. Dirty water sloshed over the rim and onto the floor. She took a deep breath and plunged under the bloodied linens. Sarah Baji had just covered Pauline up in the wicker basket when the door opened.

A Turkish officer, with black shining boots and a crisply pressed uniform held his bayonet rigid at his side as he stepped in. Behind him was Mr. Brighton, a look of sheer panic in his eyes.

Nurse Bowley was sitting beside the laundry tub, holding her abdomen as if in pain. Sarah Baji reached for the long laundry stick and stuck it into the tub, avoiding the spots where Marta and Mariam were hiding. She saw one long black braid floating on the surface of the water, so she pushed some laundry with her stick to cover it up.

The soldier walked over to the tub and looked in. His eyebrows creased in curiosity. "Did someone die in here?" he asked.

"No," said Sarah Baji, continuing to stir the laundry. Through the corner of her eye, she saw the linens in the wicker laundry basket move. She willed herself to stay calm.

The soldier's eyes were fixed on the laundry tub. "Then why all the blood?" he asked.

Sarah Baji didn't answer. Nurse Bowley sighed. The soldier looked over at her. Her face turned a bright red. "Really," she said. "It is not your business."

"Not my business?" replied the soldier, outraged. He peered back into the bloodied laundry. "Something happened here," he said.

Nurse Bowley sighed. "If you must know," she said, doubling again. "It is menstrual blood. I have been having problems with my monthly cycle. I woke up this morning in a sopping mess of menstrual blood."

The soldier's face blanched. "Oh," he said. He backed away from the laundry vat, nearly slipping in the puddle of liquid on the floor as he did so.

A minute smile formed at the corners of Mr. Brighton's mouth. He opened the door, and the officer barreled out, gagging.

As the door closed behind the two men, they could hear the soldier saying, "This building is clear."

Sarah Baji turned to look at the wicker basket just in time to see Pauline kick the clean laundry completely off herself.

Marta's forehead emerged from the bloodied water, and then her eyes. She looked frantically from Nurse Bowley to Sarah Baji, who both grinned with relief. Marta poked at Mariam to let her know it was safe, and then both women surfaced, gasping for air.

"I think it's time we both had a bath," said Mariam.

～†～

"I want to inspect all of the children in this orphanage," said the officer to Mr. Brighton as they headed away from the laundry building.

"Come with me," said Mr. Brighton quickly. "The children are all in one dormitory."

Mr. Brighton banged on the door and stepped inside. He directed the officer to the girls' section.

Nineteen little girls stood at attention, each beside their bare, metal-framed beds, their mattresses rolled in a bundle and neatly resting at the ends. The girls were dressed in coarsely woven flour sack shifts that were sleeveless and knee-length. Their feet were bare. Sheruk-rey-ah stood at the far end, beside Nadalia, her eyes round with fear. The officer walked up to each girl.

"When did you get here? Where are your parents? How old are you? What is your name?" He shot the questions out like bullets and the girls answered smartly, one by one. When he got to Sheruk-rey-ah, her hands were trembling and there were tears in her eyes. "What is your name?" he asked. "Sheruk— Par...Parantzim," she replied.

"You sound Turkish," he said.

She gulped.

"Let me see your hands."

She held them out, willing them not to shake.

He held one and examined it carefully. "This hand has not done hard work," he said. "And I see traces of henna."

He turned to Mr. Brighton. "This girl is Turkish. She comes with me. I will find her a good Turkish home."

"No!" cried Sheruk-rey-ah. "I am Armenian. Please, please, let me stay here!"

The officer was taken aback. "You would rather stay here with these dirty orphans than be placed in a loving home that I would personally select for you?"

"This is my home," said Sheruk-rey-ah. "My name is Parantzim, and I would rather die here than go with you."

The officer stepped forward and raised his hand. He slapped her across the face with such force that she fell to the ground. "Stay here and die then," he said. Then he walked out of the room.

The boys were lined up much like the girls had been, and they were also dressed in the flour-sack shifts. Only two of the boys had been at the orphanage long enough to know they had to stand at attention smartly and to keep all expressions off their faces. The officer walked up to the first urchin and said, "Wipe that smirk off your face."

The boy stopped smiling. Instead, he glared back at the officer with sheer hatred. The officer slapped him hard, drawing blood. The next boy in line got the message. He squared his shoulders and kept his face expressionless. The officer walked past him. And past the next boy. Then he stopped at Hrag. Try as he might, Hrag could not remove the look of pure hatred from his face. "What is the matter with you, boy?" asked the officer.

Hrag shrugged. The officer slapped him across the face. As if by reflex, Hrag slapped him back. The officer's face registered momentary shock, then white hot anger. "No one gets away with that," he said. He pulled out a small pistol from his belt, aimed it at Hrag's forehead, and pulled the trigger. As Hrag fell to the ground, the soldier gestured to the other boys, who were rigid with shock.

"Clean that up."

Twenty-one

KEVORK

Kevork lost track of the time. All he knew was that it was still 1916, likely November or December because the days were pleasantly cool and the nights were chilly. Every night, Kevork would sleep in the shadow of the Tarsus Mountains with his rucksack as a pillow, hugging Angele's carpet to his chest. The ground was so rocky and rough that it took him nearly five days to walk forty miles. Then the train tracks resumed. He gladly paid his ticket, sat in a booth all to himself, and looked out the window. Once, the train passed a single-file line of camels. Another time, an American in a fancy new automobile sped past.

As the train chugged toward Smyrna, Kevork took out the sunburst carpet. He threaded his shoe repair needle and tried to fix the frayed edges of Angele's beloved carpet, but his fingers were too clumsy and his thread was too thick.

As the train approached the outskirts of Smyrna, Kevork could see in the distance a fortress on top of a tall hill. When the train got closer, he saw that there were houses, mosques with minarets, mansions, and warehouses all packed tightly together at the seaport, which was at the base of the hill. The houses close to the top of the hill were built in the familiar Turkish style, with flat roofs and earthen walls, but the peak-roofed houses closer to the port were washed in bright whites or soft pinks or blues. Some of the buildings at the base of the hill had fluted white columns in front. When the train stopped, Kevork stepped down onto the platform and filled his lungs with the fresh sea air.

He walked out onto the street and was immediately accosted by a group of ragged children, speaking Greek and asking for bread. Had the Greeks been deported like the Armenians? He had heard rumors like that, but now he was seeing with his own eyes that it must be true. He had no bread to give them, but he took out a few Turkish pounds and gave them to the children.

He headed in the direction of the boulevard along the water, but the streets meandered and he ended up at an ancient ruin. Some large Grecian pillars were still standing, but others were scattered on the ground with grass growing in tufts around them. He stood in awe at the sight for just a moment, and then he went up to one of the pillars and reverently rested his hand against it. It felt pleasantly cool and solid against his palm.

Kevork retraced his steps and found the road to the boulevard along the water. Another cluster of children in threadbare clothing approached him, and again he gave them some money.

Kevork knew that Herr Bloch had rented a Greek residence along the waterfront beside the American hotel. As Kevork walked along the street looking for the American hotel, he gazed out into the harbor. Battleships mingled with fishing and cargo boats. He longed to jump on one of those vessels and sail away, far from war and hate and death.

The house beside the American hotel turned out to be an imposing stone house washed in pale yellow. It was set almost flush with the boulevard and had no courtyard. The roof was peaked and shingled in brown. There was no rope for a doorbell, so Kevork walked up to the elaborate decorated arched doorway and knocked loudly on one of the double doors. After a few moments, Kevork heard footsteps. The door opened a few inches, then opened wide. A Greek woman in a simple gray dress with a belt of keys stood there.

"Mrs. Bloch?" Kevork asked in German.

The woman's eyes wrinkled in amusement. "No," she said. "How may I help you?"

Kevork showed the woman the manila envelope. "I have come with a delivery."

The woman's expression became serious at the sight of the envelope. She took it from Kevork, examining it carefully. "Follow me," she said, ushering Kevork in with her hand.

Beyond the doors Kevork was surprised to see an enclosed courtyard after all. He followed the woman through another set of doors. Inside, the walls were whitewashed and hung with beautiful carpets in geometric designs. The floors were cool stone and in the center was a large rectangular carpet. Along two of the walls was a ledge for sitting, covered with more carpets and large cushions.

"Someone will be with you shortly," said the woman. And then she left.

Kevork didn't want to sit down. The room was too clean and he was acutely aware of how filthy he was after his long journey.

It seemed like an hour before someone finally came back into the room. The man was dressed in traditional Turkish garb, with wide trousers tight at the ankle, a plain shirt, and a short vest overtop.

"Herr Bloch?" asked Kevork.

"No," answered the man in Armenian. "I am Sarkis Gregorian. You are alone?"

"Yes," replied Kevork. And he told the man of Angele's death.

"But you were able to bring both photographs?" he asked.

"Yes," said Kevork. He unwrapped the scarf from his waist and handed Sarkis the small silk package.

The man's fingers trembled as he opened it and he gasped when he saw what it depicted. He swayed then sat down heavily on one of the cushions. "Sit, please," he said to Kevork, patting the cushion beside him.

"I am too filthy," said Kevork. He upturned his rucksack onto a table. The contents spilled out onto the floor. The prayer mat, which had been wrapped tightly around Angele's carpet remnant, tumbled out and opened.

Sarkis glanced at the beautiful green sunburst design and the ragged edges but said nothing. He watched intently as Kevork turned the rucksack inside out, then, with the leather knife, carefully ripped open the stitches at the bottom of the sack.

Kevork reached into the opening in the base of his rucksack and drew out the second silk-wrapped package. He handed it to Sarkis.

Sarkis unwrapped the second photograph and sighed. "They are both horrible," he said in a flat voice. "And only a grain of sand in the desert when compared to all that has happened in Turkey of late."

"Can you get them out of the country?" asked Kevork.

"Yes," said Sarkis. "And it will happen soon."

Kevork could feel the tension drain from his body. A wave of exhaustion coursed through him.

Sarkis stood up. "I must make the arrangements," he said. "I'll send Callista back in to show you to your room. You may stay here for as long as you wish."

A few moments after Sarkis left, the woman with the keys came in. Callista's look took in his soiled clothing and well-used rucksack. "Would you like directions to a good public bath?" she asked in German.

Kevork flushed with embarrassment. "Yes," he said.

"Let me bring you some clean clothing," she said, not unkindly. "I believe you are approximately the same size as Mr. Gregorian."

Kevork could feel the exhaustion seep through him as he sat in the steam room at the bath. When the attendant sudsed him all over and scraped him with a rough brush, Kevork felt as if a whole layer of skin had been sloughed off. He had his hair cut short and submitted to a shave. He donned Sarkis's simple shirt and trousers and looked at himself in the mirror. An unfamiliar man in Turkish dress stared back at him. He had lived so long as an Arab; now he was a Turk. Would there ever come a time when he could be himself again?

He walked back down the waterfront street to Herr Bloch's house. Callista led him past the first reception room and through a large interior courtyard—a beautiful flowering garden with fig and pomegranate trees and a small fountain with a white marble statue of a woman holding an urn. Then they went through another set of doors, up the steps, and down a hallway until they stopped at an arched wooden door. The woman took one of the keys from her belt and unlocked it. Inside was a spartan room with just the essentials: a narrow wooden bed, a washstand, a simple carpet on the floor, and a nightstand. Callista walked over to the large glass window and opened it wide. Kevork stood beside her and stared out at the spectacular view of the harbor.

"The staff eats in an hour," the woman said. "Please join us in the kitchen." She crossed the room and closed the door behind her.

Kevork lay down on the bed and was enveloped by its softness. For the first time in a long time, he felt safe.

There was no place in Turkey or Syria that wasn't touched by war, and Smyrna was no different. The city's Greek population was largely intact, but Greeks from other areas had been deported.

Many had escaped the deportation route and ended up on the streets of Smyrna. Even so, the city was far away from the deportation routes, and since it was a port, it had contact with the outside world. Kevork's refuge at Herr Bloch's rented home was as close to an oasis as one could get during wartime.

Kevork's first month at Herr Bloch's was spent recuperating. He would sit in the garden for hours, doing nothing but staring at the water trickling in the fountain. Callista would bring him a plate of food to eat out there, since he rarely joined the other servants at mealtime. And Kevork slept. His room was simple, but it was comfortable and clean.

> ⚜

While Kevork kept mostly to himself, Sarkis Gregorian spent many days away, doing errands for Herr Bloch. On one of these trips, he passed on the photos to a laundress, who passed them on to a man who to all outside appearances was a Turkish policeman. Several days later, the policeman strolled past the harbor as an American passenger ship was about to sail. A drunken American nearly fell as he stumbled to the gangplank. The policeman steadied the American by the elbow and surreptitiously slipped an envelope with the two photographs into the man's pocket as he did so.

"I'm fine, I'm fine," said John Coren, belching a blast of whiskey breath into the policeman's face.

None who witnessed the scene realized that a precious exchange had been made.

> ⚜

Kevork had nightmares almost every night for the first two weeks. He would dream that Angele was drowning. He would jump in to save her, then realize that he didn't know how to swim. He also dreamt that Marta was a piece of wood being thrown into the fire. He would jump into the flames and they would both be consumed by it, dying in agony together. He would wake up in the middle of the night, wailing like a baby. But in the morning he would feel somehow refreshed, as if he had released a demon.

Sometimes he did small chores for the household, like mending a horse harness or repairing the stitching on a shoe. He did errands too, delivering small packages to businessmen along the boulevard. But mostly he did nothing. Kevork finally met Herr Bloch, but he was rarely on the premises. It was apparent that smuggling out the photographs had been Kevork's primary purpose, and Herr Bloch was content to provide him with refuge for as long as he needed.

Months passed, then a year.

Then more months.

><((°>~

One day in late May 1918, Sarkis ran out to the garden, his eyes shining with excitement and a telegraph fluttering in his hand. Kevork stood up, his heart pounding. Was this a message about Marta?

"The best news possible!" cried Sarkis.

"It's from Marta?" asked Kevork.

"No," said Sarkis. "Armenia has declared independence!"

Kevork's jaw dropped in astonishment.

And more dreams followed.

In June, Turkey recognized the Armenian nation. And in July, Sarkis showed Kevork an American newspaper with a story about what had been happening in Turkey. It mentioned the photographs. It also mentioned that ten million dollars had been raised to aid Armenians in Turkey.

Despite his relief, Kevork's heart was empty. In all this time, there had been no news of Marta. Sarkis had sent a telegraph to the Ayguns' on Kevork's behalf, but it went unanswered. When he tried to send a telegraph to Amelia Schultz and to Miss Younger, Sarkis got a telegraph back explaining that all of the German orphanages in Turkey had been disbanded.

This news alarmed Kevork beyond imagining. If she was still alive, where would Marta go? If there was no orphanage at Marash, how would they ever find each other? He began to realize that he would have to accept the fact that he would never find her.

Twenty-two

JOHN COREN

Since Zeki's death, John had stopped drinking his whiskey by the glass. Now he took it straight from the bottle.

As he sat at the kitchen table in his parents' Boston house in the early hours of the morning, he swallowed another mouthful of whiskey. He pulled his wallet from his back pocket and shook out the contents. A flutter of papers emptied out onto the table. He unfolded one. It was a news article from a Turkish newspaper describing the spectacular fire that had engulfed the Aygun home, killing the mother, father, and apparently the child, although the body was never found. The article speculated that it may have been a suicide and double murder, since the father had been fatally ill. There was no mention of the family's underground activities.

He opened up another scrap of paper. This was one that he had found on Amelia's desk. It was similar to the one that he had ripped up so long ago: a plaintive call from Kevork for his Marta. John did not regret ripping up the first missive and he didn't regret telling Amelia not to send the second. After all, if Kevork had tried to find his Marta back then, he surely would have died. That he had been sent on an even more dangerous mission was something that John wanted to forget. But Kevork *had* survived, hadn't he? He had brought the photos all the way to Smyrna. And he was healthy and safe, according to Sarkis Gregorian's latest telegram.

That was more than he could say for the Ayguns. And look at all the good the young man had accomplished.

But times had changed. The war was turning. The allies were poised to win. Soon, Kevork would be able to travel back to Marash. Back to his beloved. That was, of course, if she were still alive.

John lived with the fact that he had not fulfilled his promise. Should he send a telegram to Mr. Brighton, the new orphanage administrator at Marash? Should he ask the man for news of Marta Hovsepian? John grabbed the bottle of whiskey and gulped down some more of the amber fluid. Yes, he should, he decided. Tomorrow. When he was sober.

Twenty-three

MARTA AND MARIAM

The months passed, and Marta settled into a routine. She would strap Pauline onto her back and continue with her chores, teaching, cooking, and helping in the laundry. Parantzim, who had now abandoned the name Sheruk-rey-ah, considered herself Pauline's godmother. When Marta needed a break, Parantzim would take the baby and find a quiet spot where she could sing the child lullabies or tell her stories.

Marta loved to see the two of them together. Even though Pauline was just a toddler, her eyes would be glued to Parantzim's as she sang or told a story. It was as if she were drinking in every word.

Both Mariam and Marta continued to live in the Rescue Home for Girls. But they were no longer isolated by hatred or disapproval. In fact, since Hrag's murder, it seemed easier to train and civilize the rescued urchins.

Parantzim decided to live in the girls' dormitory. She developed a friendship with Nadalia, and when she wasn't spending time with Pauline, the two girls could always be found together.

The days and nights blurred together in a frenzy of work and activity. Marta was glad to be busy because it took her mind off the ache in her heart. She was grateful for the fact that she had her dear baby, Pauline. But every time she looked at the girl, it reminded her of the love she had lost. And it also reminded her that even if by some miracle Kevork did return to her one day, he might reject her because of Pauline. The whole issue was too painful to dwell on, so she plunged herself into her work and tried to keep her sadness at bay.

❦

One autumn afternoon in 1918, Mr. Brighton sat down heavily at his desk. It had been a long day. The good news was that the Turkish soldiers had abandoned their posts outside the orphanage gates. The bad news was that the orphanage was being overrun— not just with the emaciated urchins, who were more than welcome, but with the regular citizens of Marash. Mr. Brighton shook his head in wonder. They would walk through the gates and look around to see what they could take. The few tables and chairs that remained were picked up and carried out. Sacks of flour, loaves of bread, dishes—anything they could get their hands on. Finally, the healthier orphans bolted the gates shut from the inside and stood watch for those who tried to climb over the gates.

Mr. Brighton held his face in his hands. He was so tired that he could fall asleep right where he sat. Something had to be happening, but what? Had the war ended? And if it had ended, who had won?

Just then, the silence was interrupted by the click-click-click of the telegraph machine. He lifted his head and watched as the paper emerged. When it was finished printing, he tore it off and grabbed his monocle to read the message. It was from the American Consulate in Syria: Turkey had capitulated. The Allies had won the war.

The exhaustion left his body in a flash. He jumped up from his chair and ran out of his office, the piece of paper trailing in his hand.

"The war has ended!" he shouted at the top of his lungs. He ran to the kitchen, where Sarah Baji was elbow-deep in dough. "The war has ended!" he cried.

Sarah Baji's hands flew out of the bread dough. She held her face in shock, covering her cheeks in the process with flour and bits of dough. Then she ran to Mr. Brighton and grabbed his shoulders. They danced around the kitchen. "Wonderful news!" she cried. Neither of them took any notice of the white flour marks all over everywhere.

Mr. Brighton ran out of the kitchen and to the classroom. Marta, who was at the chalkboard with Pauline strapped to her back, blinked in shock at the absurd sight of Mr. Brighton, wild-eyed and covered with flour.

"The war is over!" he cried. "Our side won!"

The children screamed with excitement and began jumping and dancing and singing for joy. "Class dismissed!" cried Marta. Then she ran out of the classroom, close on Mr. Brighton's heels.

Mariam was in the infirmary with Nurse Bowley, where they were looking after some of the less fortunate urchins who had just arrived. Mariam was spoon-feeding one little boy when her sister rushed in. She almost dropped the bowl of soup in her astonishment at the news.

"Wonderful!" she cried.

Twenty-four

KEVORK

Kevork had been sitting in Herr Bloch's garden on a cool autumn evening, slowly plowing through a dry German novel when he heard the news. It was one of the rare occasions that Kevork had seen Herr Bloch himself. The businessman came into the garden and sat down on a wrought-iron chair beside Kevork and stared into the fountain for a moment, a crease of worry on his face.

He said, "The war has ended."

The statement was given in such a quiet fashion that Kevork didn't know how to respond. He waited a moment, hoping that Herr Bloch would say more. After a minute of silence, Herr Bloch spoke again. "I will be closing this house and going back to Germany. You and Sarkis will have to leave."

Kevork's heart sank. Did this mean that Turkey and Germany had won? What would happen to him now? He dared not even imagine.

"The Young Turk leaders, Djemal, Enver, and Talaat, have fled to Germany," continued Herr Bloch.

"What?" cried Kevork in surprise.

Herr Bloch regarded Kevork with curiosity. "The Allies won, you know."

Kevork felt like jumping for joy. He felt like hugging Herr

177

Bloch. "I didn't know," he said. He stopped himself from saying more. After all, it was the best news for Armenians, but not for German businessmen like Herr Bloch.

"Do you know where you will go?" asked Herr Bloch.

"No," replied Kevork. And that was the sad part. Where *could* he go, after all? When you are the only survivor, there is no going home.

⤝╍╤╍⤜

That night, Kevork and Sarkis went out to a taverna to celebrate. It was a raucous place, with Greek and Armenian refugees singing and crying and getting drunk. Deep into the night, the air became heavy with cigarette smoke and the licorice scent of ouzo, the Greek liqueur. Kevork and Sarkis linked arms with the other men and danced the traditional Greek line dance, kicking and shouting in step, snaking in between the taverna tables and then out onto the street.

As they finally headed back to Herr Bloch's house, Kevork asked, "Do you know where you're going to go?"

"Yerevan," answered Sarkis. "I don't care how long it takes me to get there, but I want to be part of the new Armenia."

The new Armenia. A fresh start. What could be better than that? "Don't you have anyone to go home to?" asked Kevork.

Sarkis stopped walking for a moment and looked at Kevork with deep sadness. "I don't know," he said. "But it is doubtful."

Kevork knew exactly what he meant. He had witnessed his sister's murder. And he knew that his father had died because he had received a letter about it. And he was with Angele when she died. But what about Marta? Or his own mother? How would he ever find out? "Perhaps I should go to Yerevan too," said Kevork.

Sarkis didn't exactly smile, but the sadness in his eyes diminished just a bit. "That is a very good idea," he said. "We could go together."

A few days later, Kevork opened up his rucksack and began to sort it out. He still had his awl, his leather knife, and his other shoemaking tools from Aleppo, so he wrapped them carefully and packed them up. Then he unwrapped a familiar bundle. It was his prayer mat wrapped over the frayed and fragile portion of the beautiful green sunburst carpet that Angele had been making before she died. He hadn't taken it out since arriving at Herr Bloch's; there had been no need to pretend he was Muslim inside the house.

He picked up the carpet piece and held it to his face. Then he traced the geometric sunburst design with one finger. "I will get you to freedom, Angele," he said softly. He rewrapped it in the prayer mat and tucked it carefully into his rucksack.

Herr Bloch had bought enough good leather for Kevork to make them each a sturdy pair of traveling boots, and he gave both Sarkis and Kevork a generous stipend, a mixture of German francs and American dollars.

"I cannot guarantee that this will get you all the way to Yerevan," said Herr Bloch. "But if you spend wisely, you should get there and still have a little bit to spare."

Kevork shook Herr Bloch's hand one last time and then he and Sarkis walked to the train station.

Only days after they left, a telegram arrived for Kevork, care of Herr Bloch. It was from John Coren in Boston. Herr Block cursed as he read it. If only it could have arrived a few days earlier! The telegram announced that Marta Hovsepian had been found alive and well in the American orphanage in Marash.

"It is out of my hands," Herr Bloch whispered to himself. "If only there were something I could do to let Kevork know."

He packed up his things and left the next day for Germany. But just before his departure, Her Bloch sent a telegraph to Kevork, care of the new Armenian administration in Yerevan, telling of Marta's survival. He could only hope that Kevork would get the message one day.

Twenty-five

MARTA AND MARIAM

Within weeks of Turkey's defeat, a contingent of Canadian and American missionaries arrived at the orphanage in Marash, headed up by an American physician, Dr. Helen Thomas.

Dr. Thomas cut a strange figure in a world where many women were completely covered in a chador and others were covered from neck to ankle. Instead of a white blouse and long dark skirt, the standard female missionary dress, Dr. Thomas sported a suit tailored like a man's but with a narrow skirt that shockingly stopped at mid-calf. And she wore shoes, not boots. Marta often found herself staring at Dr. Thomas' ankles. For a long while, she thought that they were bare, but then she realized that the doctor was wearing a kind of sheer flesh-toned stocking.

The nurses who accompanied Dr. Thomas also wore calf-length outfits, but theirs were dark skirts and blouses with a white wrap-around smock over top. And they wore a white veil that covered all but the front of their hair. These strange new beings took over the running of the orphanage.

Both Marta and Mariam found themselves in great demand as interpreters. The new missionaries did not speak either Armenian or Turkish well.

Mariam's life changed dramatically with the end of the war. When she wasn't interpreting for Dr. Thomas or the nurses, she was organizing the children into work squadrons. Some of the groups were assigned donated clothing from North America. Each group had their specialty: one would rework women's dresses into tunics, while another would organize and repair sets of shoes. Other squadrons specialized in making underwear and trousers. Dr. Thomas had also brought with her knitting machines and yarn, so one squadron was taught to make stockings.

Mr. Brighton stayed on at the orphanage as second in command, but he felt almost useless beside the formidable Dr. Helen Thomas. He could assist, but he wanted to do more. One day, at the end of a very busy day, he sat down beside Mariam after dinner in the dining hall. "I have a plan, and I need your help," he said.

She set down her cup of tea and said, "Anything I can do to help, you know I will."

"Look around you," he said, gesturing to the many children, and the occasional elderly woman or man. "The young men are mostly dead. We know that," said Mr. Brighton, "but what about the women?"

Mariam knew exactly what he meant. While the deportations and massacres had been a government plan to rid Turkey of Armenians, it was mostly targeted at the men. The married older women and men had died of starvation and exposure rather than outright killing. But the girls and young Armenian women, especially the attractive ones, had not all been killed. Many had been taken into Turkish homes. They were forced to adopt the Muslim faith and were used as slaves and extra wives. Many of the young healthy Armenian boys also escaped death. They were valued because they were young enough to forget their heritage. They were raised as Turkish sons.

"The future of the Armenian nation depends on rescuing

these young women and boys from Turkish homes," he said. "You could interpret for them and for me."

"Yes. I will help you with that," she replied.

Mr. Brighton visited the offices of the transitional government, which had been set up by the Allies after the Young Turks had been thrown out of power. He obtained official documents that permitted him to rescue any Armenian found in a Turkish home.

In addition to all of the other modern amenities Dr. Thomas and her crew had brought from America was an automobile. Mr. Brighton assured Mariam that he knew how to drive, and so, armed with their official papers, they set off one day, just as the early morning call to prayer had finished.

Mariam felt odd, covered up in the chador that she hadn't worn since leaving Rustem's home, but she realized that they would have a better reception at Muslim homes if she were dressed this way.

"Where do we start?" Mariam asked as the automobile weaved its way through the streets, avoiding vendors with baskets, beggars on the ground, and stray dogs.

"Let us start in the wealthiest district first," said Mr. Brighton, slamming on the brakes to avoid hitting a woman in a chador walking her goat down the middle of the road.

Mariam nodded in agreement. The wealthier families would have the financial resources to support extra women. The poorest Muslim husbands usually only had a single wife.

As they pulled up to a large stucco house in the old Turkish district, Mariam looked up to the latticed windows on the second floor. A pair of eyes stared back at her.

Mariam and Mr. Brighton walked together to the main entrance of the house. He pulled the bell rope, and when a man answered the door, Mr. Brighton looked expectantly to Mariam. It took her a moment to realize that it was she who would be doing the talking. It seemed that just wearing the chador again had transformed her into a quieter, more submissive version of herself.

"I...I...we—," she stuttered in Turkish.

"If you are selling something, I am not interested," said the man. He began to close the door.

"No," said Mariam, regaining her equilibrium. She grabbed the document from Mr. Brighton's hands. "This is an order from the government," she said. "You must relinquish any Armenian woman or child who lives here."

"No Armenian lives here," said the man. He slammed the door.

"That didn't work very well," said Mariam as they walked down the street to the next house.

They tried a few more houses, but they had no more success than with the first one. They were about to give up when Mariam had an idea. "Take me to the market," she said.

Mr. Brighton gave her an odd look, but did as she requested. In the market, she haggled with a few vendors until she had a substantial variety of beads and baubles and pretty ribbons. She also bought a decorative wicker basket with a big looped carrying handle. Once she got back into the car, she sorted out her goods in a pleasing fashion. Then she took the government document from Mr. Brighton and tucked it into the folds of her chador.

"Let's try another street," she said.

Mr. Brighton drove to one of the oldest areas of the city, where the cobblestone streets were narrow and winding. Some of the houses were centuries old and were built so close to each other that they shared walls. "Wait here for me," she said.

Mr. Brighton parked the car at the end of the street, and

Mariam exited, the wicker basket resting in the crook of her arm. She rapped her knuckle on the first door she came to, then waited. A man answered.

"What do you want?" he asked in Turkish.

"The ladies of the house might be interested in my wares," answered Mariam.

The man glanced briefly at her and then at the contents of her basket. "Wait in here," he said, ushering her into a room just beyond the front door. There was low table in the middle of the room and a sitting ledge adorned with ornately decorated cushions. The floors and walls were covered with showy woven carpets. Mariam stood nervously in one corner, clutching her wicker basket in front of her.

A few moments passed, and then a woman, bent and heavy with age and covered entirely in black, walked in. "What do you have?" asked the woman. Her eyes were drawn to the colorful baubles in the basket. The woman ran a rough hand through the selection, then looked up at Mariam. "Cheap trinkets," she said. "But Karli might like them. Wait here."

Mariam breathed a sigh of relief as the woman left. Would her ploy work? A few minutes passed, and the waiting made Mariam weak at the knees with anxiety, so she perched at the edge of one of the sofas. Finally a young woman holding a baby in her arms entered the room. Karli was wearing a colorful Turkish house-dress, and her face was uncovered. Her arms and neck were thin and pale, but her baby was dimpled with ripples of fat. She sat down beside Mariam and set the baby on her lap, but he squirmed at the sight of the colorful beads and lunged toward the basket, nearly falling right in.

"Careful, Ibrahim," said the girl, looping her arm around his waist and pulling him back onto her lap.

"This would look lovely in your hair," said Mariam in Turkish, holding up a shiny green ribbon.

The girl took the ribbon with her free hand and examined it carefully. "It *is* lovely," she said. "Yes, I shall take it."

"And what about this necklace?" asked Mariam in Armenian as she held out a dainty choker made of silver seed beads.

"That is lovely too," answered Karli in Armenian. "I think I—" Then she stopped. Her eyes opened wide and she tilted her head, giving Mariam an odd look. Her eyes darted to the door that led to the rest of the house. It was opened a crack, so she hoisted the squirming baby to her hip, walked over to the door, and shut it firmly.

She sat back down beside Mariam and whispered, "Are you Armenian?"

"Yes," answered Mariam in a low voice.

"I heard the war has ended," Karli said.

"It has," said Mariam. "The Young Turks have fled. The new Sultan is working with the Allies, and the Armenians are now safe."

The girl's eyes filled with tears. "I need to get out of here."

"I can help you," said Mariam. Then she pulled out the official document from the folds of her chador. "Your husband is legally required to relinquish you."

Karli's lower lip trembled. "He is going to be very angry." Then she looked at the child on her lap and tears spilled down her cheeks. "He will not allow me to take Ibrahim. I know that."

"I have an idea," said Mariam. "Come with me right now. There is a car waiting outside. You don't have to tell anyone."

Karli covered her mouth with her free hand and her eyes widened in surprise. "Can I do that?" she asked.

"You are free to go," said Mariam. Then she grabbed her basket of trinkets and walked quickly to the door. Karli followed close behind, both arms wrapped tightly around her squirming son. They were out the door and halfway down the street when the elderly woman dashed out the front door.

"Come back here, Karli!" she called. "You cannot kidnap my grandson!"

Mr. Brighton saw the two women run down the street, so he started the car. Mariam opened the passenger door and shoved Karli and the baby in. Then she scampered in beside them, slamming the door shut just as Mr. Brighton put the car in reverse and backed away from the street. He turned the car around and jammed his foot down on the gas. Suddenly, they heard a pounding on the back of the car. Mariam turned around and saw the man who had opened the door for her earlier. His eyes were fiery with anger and he pounded his fists on the trunk of the car.

"Stop the car! Karli, I demand that you get out of the car!"

The wheels spun, loosening dust from between the cobbles, and then the car shot forward. The man ran after them, but he gave up after a block or two. The last image Mariam had was of the man standing in the middle of the road with his feet planted shoulder-width apart, shaking his fist at them.

As they drove off, Karli hugged her baby tight on her lap. "Thank you," she said. "I baptized my little boy Apraham in secret," she said. "And I prayed that I could raise him Armenian."

⚓

The arrival of the army of helpers was a huge relief to Marta and the rest. They had all been working nonstop and with little resources since the Allies' victory. Hundreds of new orphans streamed in each day. So many of them had nothing. They wore shreds of rags and were covered with sores and lice. Their arms and legs were like fragile sticks, and their eyes were sad. But what was even worse was that each one was alone in the world. Each one had lost a family, but many did not even have the memory of their family to comfort them. It made Marta grateful that she had Pauline, and it made her loathe to be apart from her, even for a few minutes.

But as more and more orphans poured through the gates, Marta realized that it would be foolhardy for her to continue to keep Pauline with her at all times. Contagion was in the air: typhus, cholera, tuberculosis. The few adults were vastly outnumbered by the orphans, so there was much work to do.

The new missionaries insisted that Pauline and the other healthy children be kept separate from the new arrivals. Reluctantly, during the workday, Marta relinquished Pauline to the missionaries in charge of the healthy children. They set up a nursery with games and activities, and while two-year-old Pauline loved it, Marta felt bereft without her. Each night, her heart was filled with joy when she and Pauline were reunited. They would share a narrow cot, Marta's arms wrapped protectively around her daughter.

A number of elderly women also found their way to the orphanage. Marta searched each of their faces as they arrived, hoping against hope that Anahid Baji, her own grandmother, had somehow survived.

One day, a tiny woman who called herself Voskie Baji came to the orphanage. She was shriveled like an old apple, and she had with her two emaciated little boys who clung to her with loving desperation. She did not look at all like Marta's own grandmother, but there was something in her fierce dedication to the two boys that was so familiar. Marta gave them each a piece of flat bread to eat and then she called to one of the nurses to help her.

"Take the children and bathe them," she said. Then she added gently, "And I will look after Voskie Baji myself."

The grandmother was loathe to be parted from the two boys, and they wailed to see her go in a different direction. But Marta assured her that they would be looked after and reunited shortly.

Marta took the old woman to a washing station that had been set up in the women's area of the orphanage. She helped Voskie Baji unwrap her rags, using tongs to avoid the hundreds of lice. She threw the writhing cloth into the incinerator and shaved the woman's scalp. She helped the old woman into a tub filled with clean, warm water. As she handed Voskie Baji a bar of soap, tears sprang in the old woman's eyes.

"Thank you, daughter," she said. "You are so kind."

Marta's throat filled with tears. The poor woman had been through so much, yet she was so gracious, so thankful. Marta lathered soap on the woman's head, gently massaging her scalp as if she still had hair, being careful not to get soap in her eyes. When she was finished, Marta gave Voskie Baji an outfit that had been fashioned out of the used clothing sent from abroad. Voskie Baji grinned toothlessly as she looked down at herself, decked out in a brown striped blouse and a red polka-dotted skirt. "It feels so good to be clean," she said.

Marta took the woman to her grandsons. They found the boys standing on either side of the nurse, a forlorn look in their eyes. Like their grandmother, they had also been shaved. One was wearing a pink tunic and the other was in a gray floral tunic. When they saw their grandmother, their faces lit up and they ran to her, hugging her knees tight.

These boys are lucky, thought Marta. They are a family. And it made her think of her little brother Onnig. Had he survived? He would be thirteen now. She wondered if she would ever see him again, or even recognize him if she did.

Over time, Mr. Brighton and Mariam became adept at saving Armenian women and children from Turkish homes. Soon the Rescue Home for Girls was filled.

During one of their outings, Mr. Brighton pointed out a prosperous-looking mansion in one of the newer districts. "We haven't gone there yet," he commented.

"There are no Armenians in that house," said Mariam.

"How can you be certain?" Mr. Brighton asked.

"Because it is Rustem Bey's home, and that is where I stayed."

"Ah," said Mr. Brighton. "So this is where the good Rustem Bey lives." Rustem was known throughout the orphanage as a fine and honorable man. Not only had he given refuge to Mariam and Parantzim with no strings attached, but he had continued to keep the orphanage supplied throughout the war, even though by doing so, he risked his life.

"Would you like to stop in anyway?" asked Mr. Brighton.

It seemed an audacious thing to do, to call on Rustem. It was not ladylike, but then again, how ladylike was it to go from house to house, rescuing Armenians?

"I would like that," she said.

Mr. Brighton parked the car and they both walked up to Rustem's house. As she pulled on the bell-rope, Mariam's heart fluttered. She didn't know whether it fluttered with joy or dread, excitement or anticipation. The manservant who answered did not recognize her. But then, how could he? Only her eyes showed through the chador.

"We are here to see Rustem Bey," said Mr. Brighton in his ungrammatical Turkish.

The servant looked Mr. Brighton up and down as if trying to

figure him out, and then he regarded Mariam with curiosity. "This way," he said.

As he led them into the receiving room she knew so well, Mariam breathed in the familiar scent of sandalwood and musk. She sat down on the edge of a circular sofa in the middle of the room. The house had not exactly been a home to her, but it had been a welcome refuge. She felt a sense of longing, even a twinge of remorse. She had not been happy here, and Rustem's mother had certainly treated her poorly, but Rustem himself had always acted with brotherly respect and compassion. Was her heart telling her that she missed him?

Just then, Rustem walked in. Mariam was struck by how handsome he was. She had never really noticed that before. Even when he had proposed to her, she'd had never thought of him as anything more than a friend. But now he looked older and more serious, more grounded somehow. He looked with bored politeness at Mr. Brighton and held out his hand. Then his eye caught hers.

"Mariam?" he asked, surprised.

She stood up and removed the head covering of her chador, shaking her long braid of hair free. "Hello, Rustem," she said. "It is good to see you."

"Sit," he said. Then he looked from Mariam to Mr. Brighton, who still stood.

"I would like to talk to Rustem in private," said Mariam to Mr. Brighton.

He nodded. "I will wait for you in the car," he said.

Once the door behind Mr. Brighton clicked shut, Rustem turned to Mariam. "Have you decided to come back to me?" he asked.

"No," said Mariam. "I was in the area…" As the words left her, she realized how unlikely that sounded. And the truth of the matter was that she had missed him. She started again. "If times were different," she said, "perhaps it would have worked out between you and me."

"Halah Mustapha has gone back to her family," said Rustem abruptly.

Mariam blinked in surprise. She knew all along that the arranged marriage had been foisted upon Rustem by his conniving mother, but it never occurred to her that Halah would have been just as unhappy. "But she was with child," said Mariam.

"A healthy and beautiful little girl," said Rustem, smiling for the first time. "Her name is Guluzar." The smile vanished. "After my mother."

"Did she take the girl with her?" asked Mariam.

"No," he replied. "She left her behind."

"Oh!" said Mariam. How unusual. It was Turkish custom that all children went with the mother, but when a son turned twelve, he would leave his mother's house and live with his father. It was one of the main problems she had encountered while rescuing Armenian women. Many of them did not want to leave their Turkish husbands for fear of being cut off from their sons.

"And is your mother well?" Mariam asked dryly.

"My mother is disgustingly healthy," said Rustem. "And she takes great delight in her little granddaughter. But the last topic I wish to discuss with you is my mother." This was said with a slight smile.

"What would you like to discuss?" Mariam asked.

"I want you to marry me," said Rustem.

"Rustem," Mariam sighed. "It wouldn't work, and you know it. I could never live under the same roof as your mother. And I could never live as a Muslim."

"What if we left Turkey?" said Rustem. "We could go to South America, or maybe Canada."

Mariam reached out and took one of Rustem's hands in both of her own. "I need to stay here and help with the orphans," she said.

"Is there someone else?" he asked.

"There are the orphans," she said, a pleading look in her eyes.

"But what about a man in your life?" he asked.

Mariam didn't answer right away. The reality was that the Armenian men were mostly dead, but even so, there never had been any man she had ever liked as much as she liked Rustem. It was hard for her to admit, even to herself, that she might love him. She felt herself blushing, and looked down at her feet.

Rustem put his finger under her chin and gently raised her face so he could look her in the eye. "*Is* there someone else?" he asked again.

"No," she said. "There has never been any other man."

He kissed her on the lips. She blinked in surprise.

"Then I shall wait for you," he said.

Mariam felt tears catch in her throat.

"Come to me anytime, Mariam," he said. "And we will go away together."

Twenty-six

KEVORK

Kevork and Sarkis left early for the train station, but the place was swarming with people. Greek and Armenian refugees were trying to get back to their homes in mainland Turkey, and Turkish soldiers were traveling home from the front. People pushed and shoved and screamed as they waited in a long, snaking lineup at the lone ticket booth. Finally, the ticket agent closed his window in exasperation.

"I think we should walk," said Kevork. After all, he was used to walking. He felt as if he had walked the whole countryside of Turkey already.

And so they set out.

They stuck to the path of the railway tracks as much as they could. They were not alone. In front of them for many of the first miles were three Armenian boys and a very young girl. They were all in rags and it was hard to know if they were related or simply brought together by fate, but the boys took turns carrying the little girl in their arms or on their back. When they finally rested and Kevork and Sarkis passed them, Kevork handed the oldest boy an American dollar.

The boy's eyes sparkled in appreciation. "Thank you!" he breathed.

Much later, they passed a man in a ragged Turkish Army uniform. His left leg was amputated above the knee, and he was making good progress with his homemade crutches. But he had to rest frequently. As they passed him, Sarkis reached into his rucksack. The man cowered, perhaps thinking that Sarkis had a weapon. But when Sarkis pulled out a piece of dried bread and handed it to him, the man grinned toothlessly. "Allah is good," he said.

It was chilly in the evenings, but Kevork and Sarkis both preferred to sleep under the open stars. They took turns, one tending the fire and keeping an eye out for hostile strangers, while the other slept. Kevork enjoyed having the company of Sarkis on the trip.

When they reached the green valley where Kevork had buried Angele, they stopped for the night. Kevork spread Angele's green sunburst carpet beside her grave. As he slept on the carpet, he dreamt that she was still alive. "Armenia is free," he said. And in his dream, she smiled at him and nodded. "Go find Marta," she said. Yes, he thought…find Marta. But where?

The days of travel became weeks, and Kevork lost track of time. It was difficult to find food to buy along the way. The few farmers' fields they passed had been picked clean by others before them. Even when they came to a town, supplies were rare and expensive. So they decided to abandon the railway tracks and head due east along the old dirt roads instead.

One morning, while Kevork and Sarkis broke their morning fast with a bit of dried fruit and some water, Kevork asked Sarkis, "Where did you live before the deportations?"

"In Sis," answered Sarkis.

Kevork looked at him in surprise. Sis had been the ancient capital of the Armenian Kingdom of Cilicia. It was a village that every Armenian knew about. "That is on our route to Yerevan," he said.

"I know," said Sarkis. He picked up a dried apricot from the palm of his hand and put it in his mouth. He chewed slowly and said no more.

Kevork didn't say that he had walked through Sis himself as a child. It was halfway between his small birthplace on the Adana Plain and his later home in Marash.

They could see the ancient fort of Sis high up on the hillside long before they got there. Sarkis became moody and strange the closer they got.

"Whether you like it or not, we must visit your old home," said Kevork.

Sarkis didn't answer. He walked on.

The vast plain of the Adana region opened up in front of them. As they approached Sis, the ground angled downward and they had a breathtaking view of the whole city.

"We had a farm that way," said Sarkis, pointing to the east of Sis. He continued walking.

He stopped when they got to a low stone house with chickens running free. Near it was an apricot orchard and a small field that had been recently planted with a winter crop of barley.

They trudged on and Kevork watched Sarkis blinking back his tears. Kevork said nothing, but he could see the indecision in his friend's face. Could his family still be living there? Had they somehow survived the deportations? The house had certainly looked lived in.

Abruptly Sarkis turned and ran up to the door. Pushing it open, he called, "Mairig? Are you there?"

No answer.

Kevork waited in the yard while Sarkis ran behind the house and called again, "Mairig?"

A shrill woman's scream.

Kevork ran to the back of the house. There stood a young

woman in a Turkish housedress, her sleeves rolled up to her elbow and her forearms covered with suds. She stood beside a wooden tub in which a naked old woman sat, her long breasts half immersed in water.

"What do you want?" the young woman asked in Turkish. She grabbed a towel and did her best to hide the old woman's nakedness.

"This is my house," said Sarkis, indicating the whole farm with a wave of his hand.

The young woman shook her head. "No," she said.

Sarkis's hand fell to his side. "Did you know the Gregorians?" he asked in Turkish.

"The Armenians who used to live here?" she asked.

"Yes," he said.

"I never met them," she said.

"I am their son."

Her eyes widened with shock. She looked from Sarkis to Kevork and then to the old woman in the tub. Her eyes filled with tears. "Please don't hurt us," she said.

Sarkis sighed. "I don't want to hurt you," he said.

"Let me finish bathing Büyükanne Baji," she said. "And then we can talk."

Kevork and Sarkis went around to the front of the house and leaned up against its stone wall. They waited in silence.

A few minutes passed, and then the front door opened. The grandmother stood there, dressed all in black, with the bottom half of her face covered. She held out a carpet.

"Neylan Hanim is preparing some food for you," she said in Turkish. "It would be unseemly to invite you in, but here is a carpet for you to sit on."

Kevork took the carpet from the old woman and spread it out on the ground in front of the house.

When Neylan Hanim came out bearing a tray of fruit, bread, and tall glasses of tan, she too was wearing a chador. She set the tray down on the middle of the carpet and went back into the house. A moment later, she was at the door, struggling to get a high-backed wooden chair through the doorframe.

Sarkis jumped up to help her. "Büyükanne Baji has bad knees," she explained. "She cannot sit on the carpet."

Once the chair was out in the sunlight, Sarkis inhaled sharply. He recognized the chair. His father had carved it himself, assembling it with care. Sarkis's own grandmother would use it because of her knees.

Neylan Hanim saw Sarkis's expression and surmised the reason. "Büyükanne Baji is a kind woman," she said.

Sarkis went back to the carpet and sat down. He ripped off a bit of fresh flat bread and brought it to his mouth, but he set it down again.

The old woman saw his actions and said in Turkish, "I knew your family."

Sarkis looked up at the old woman and searched her face. Was there hardness there? No.

"They did not survive," she said gently. "But they didn't suffer as much as some of the others."

Sarkis swallowed hard and a single tear rolled down his face. "How did you end up in our house?" he asked the old woman.

"My son was in the army," said the woman. "This house was given to him by the government."

"Where is your son now?" he asked.

"Dead," she said. "All of my sons are dead. They were drafted into the Turkish Army. They were not given weapons to fight or proper clothing. All of the Turkish men of this district are just as dead as the Armenians."

"And you?" asked Sarkis, turning to the young widow. Then he saw that her shoulders were shaking through the chador. He heard a suppressed sob.

Then she said, in Armenian, "Büyükanne Baji's son saved me from deportation. He married me and treated me well as long as he lived."

The grandmother reached down and patted the girl on the shoulder. "You are a good girl," she said.

They finished their repast in silence. When they were finished, Kevork got up. "Thank you for your hospitality," he said. He slung his rucksack over his shoulder and looked down at Sarkis expectantly.

But Sarkis didn't move.

"Are you coming?" asked Kevork.

"No," replied Sarkis. "You will have to go to Yerevan without me. This is my home."

Kevork looked from Sarkis to the young girl and the grandmother. Neither of the women seemed to be particularly surprised by Sarkis's statement.

Then the grandmother said to Kevork, "You are welcome to stay here too."

⤜╪⤛

Kevork stayed the night, sleeping under the stars beside Sarkis and with Angele's carpet close to his face. When he awoke, he found that he was clasping the wedding ring in his hand. He hadn't remembered taking it off. In fact, he hadn't really thought about the wedding ring for a long time.

Sarkis had woken long before Kevork and was sitting on the roof, hammering in a loose wooden shingle. When he saw that Kevork had finally risen, he jumped off the roof. He held out a sweat-drenched hand and said, "I am sorry to be parted from you, friend. But it is my destiny to stay here."

Kevork nodded. "Be well," he said. And then he slung his rucksack over one shoulder. He was about to leave when Neylan Hanim ran out of the house with a cloth packet in her hands.

"Take this," she said. "It is food for your journey."

Kevork took the packet with thanks and then began walking east.

⚜

Marash was only forty or so miles northeast of Sis—a two-day walk if luck was on Kevork's side. And Marash was directly on the road to Yerevan, so Kevork would have to pass through it. He was almost afraid. It had upset him to see what had become of his birth village in Adana. What would Marash, the city of Marta's birth, look like now? Sometimes it was better to simply forget.

As he approached the familiar carved lions guarding the city gates of Marash, he remembered the last time he had seen them. Marta had been at his side, dressed as a boy. And they'd had the point of a bayonet at their backs. But now the lions seemed to welcome him. Or perhaps it was a mirage. Maybe what he really needed was a mouthful of water.

As he stepped through the gates, he reached into his rucksack and took out some of his American dollar bills. His plan was to give a dollar to each urchin he saw until his handful ran out. He looked at the sidewalks and the doorsteps and behind the stoops, but there were no bone-thin urchins, huddled together in rags, staring back at him. He had become so used to the sight in the past few years that their absence confused him.

As he walked on, tucking his fistful of cash into his trouser pocket, he almost stumbled over a man lying in the gutter. Kevork looked down at him in surprise. The man was wearing a thread-bare Turkish Army uniform, but his trousers were folded back above the knee. Both legs had been amputated.

"Let me help you out of this," said Kevork, gripping the man under his armpits and dragging him off the road. He set the man upright, out of the way of foot traffic and leaning against the stone wall of a coffee house.

"Thank you," said the man forlornly, blinking back tears. "Can you spare a lira for a war veteran?" he asked in a wavering voice.

Kevork pulled out several of the dollar bills from his trouser pocket and handed them to the man. "Allah is good," said the soldier.

Kevork wondered what this soldier had seen and where he had fought. Why wasn't he being cared for now? Perhaps he had been to the front, and not on the deportation operations. For the most part, the *zaptiehs* (mercenaries) who had helped with the deportation operations had not been regular Turkish soldiers at all, but criminals let out of prisons and issued secondhand uniforms. This man was probably nothing more than a village man, like Kevork himself. Perhaps he was even from the old Turkish section of his own village. Yet fate had decided that this man and Kevork must be enemies.

Fate was strange.

Kevork walked on and encountered another begging soldier, this one without an arm. The abandoned Turkish soldiers now seemed to be as plentiful as the urchins used to be. Kevork distributed the dollar bills from his pocket, reached into his rucksack, and pulled out a few more. He didn't want to give them all away because he still had a long way to go to get to Yerevan and the new republic of Armenia. But he couldn't stand to see these poor men who had nothing. It also made Kevork wonder about the Young

Turk Government. He had thought that they hated Armenians alone, but while in Smyrna, he realized that the deportations were also directed against the Greeks. Now he could see that even the lives of Turkish soldiers were cheap. What had been dear to the Young Turk Government, Kevork wondered? Thank God they had been ousted. He could only hope that a more compassionate government was in control now.

He walked on, breathing in the familiar aroma of coffee and spices as he passed the open market. It was a welcome scent and he filled his lungs with it, but it only partly masked the stench of decaying flesh. He continued on until he got to what used to be the Armenian section of Marash. He walked down the cobbled winding street until he got to Marta's childhood home. The stone wall in front of the courtyard came to Kevork's chin, so his stood on his toes and looked over it and into the yard. The same apricot, fig, and almond trees were there, only taller and bushier, and there was a goat tethered to the almond tree.

He looked into the small glass window beside the front door of the house. When Marta's family had lived here, the glass was open, but now it was covered with a delicately carved wooden lattice. A woman's face, covered but for her eyes, stared out at him through the latticework. Marta's family couldn't possibly live there anymore. He sighed with resignation. But really, what had he expected? That part of his life was over.

He trudged on through the weaving streets of Marash and, hardly knowing where he was going, he ended up at the gates of his old orphanage. Two American soldiers were sitting at a small portable table in front of the gate. They were playing cards. Kevork walked up to them and asked in English, "What is this place now?"

One of the soldiers looked up from his hand and regarded Kevork. "Why, the orphanage," he said. "What else would it be?"

"The German orphanage?" asked Kevork? "I had been told it was closed down."

"The Germans left some time ago," said the soldier. "The Near East Relief runs it now."

"Near East Relief?" asked Kevork.

"Yes," said the soldier. "When people in the U.S., Canada, and Britain saw what was happening to the Armenians here, they raised millions of dollars. The hospital in there," the soldier pointed to the gate with his hand of cards, "is as good as any in America."

Kevork knew that foreigners had been sending money for quite some time. Wasn't it foreign money that had allowed him to travel through the concentration camps, giving relief where he could? And wasn't it foreign money that helped supply the safe houses? But the effort was much bigger now. His heart pounded in his chest with excitement and sudden anxiety. Finally, he said, "Is it possible for me to go into the orphanage compound?"

"That depends," said the soldier. "Who are you?"

"I am Kevork Adomian, the shoemaker," he replied.

"You're Armenian?" the soldier asked.

Kevork nodded.

"We don't get many Armenian men here," said the soldier suspiciously. "Especially not healthy ones. You look Arab to me, with those tattoos," continued the soldier.

"Do you want me to prove that I am Christian?" said Kevork. He set his rucksack on the ground and began to unbuckle his belt.

"No, no," said the soldier, alarmed. "I believe you." Then he set his hand of cards down on the table and stood up. "Go on inside," he said, unlocking the gate.

Kevork's jaw dropped at the sight that greeted him when he stepped inside the orphanage gates. In the huge courtyard where ball games would be played or assemblies would be conducted were thousands of urchins. But they weren't huddled together in rags; they were being processed. In front of Kevork stood a long table set up with a series of boxes. Children were lined up in rows at the table. They were clean, their heads shaven, and they were all wearing tunics that were similar in style but in an astonishing array of colorful fabrics. At the head of each line stood a woman dressed in a white skirt and blouse, with white stockings and shoes, and a white veil on her head. To Kevork, they looked like a row of angels. They were examining the children one by one, marking down notes on cards, and filing the cards in the boxes on the table.

Beyond these children, Kevork could see another group. These had obviously not been there as long. They were being stripped of their clothing, and their discarded rags were being thrown into a huge bonfire. Another group of children were being shaved, and yet another group were bathing together.

So this is where all of the urchins had gone.

Kevork walked past the various groups of children unnoticed by the nurses and the other uniformed adults. When he reached the other side of the courtyard, he found himself in front of what used to be Miss Younger's door. He knocked. It was opened by a bald man with a monocle.

"Hello, hello," said the man, holding out his hand to Kevork. "My name is Mr. Brighton, and who are you?"

Kevork pressed his own hand firmly into that of Mr. Brighton's. "I am Kevork Adomian, the shoemaker," he replied.

"A shoemaker!" exclaimed Mr. Brighton. "And Armenian! We don't see too many adult Armenian males here," he said. "Are you wanting refuge?"

Kevork blinked in surprise. Refuge? "No," he said. "I am on my way to Yerevan."

"That is too bad," said Mr. Brighton. "The little ones here could use an Armenian father figure."

Kevork smiled at the thought. A father figure? But then he looked around. The children were so young. So fragile. "I also wanted to enquire about whether you have ever received news about my betrothed," said Kevork.

Mr. Brighton sighed. "One can always hope. Come into my office, and I will check my files."

Little had changed in the office since Miss Younger had been the administrator before the war. The desk was the same and the chairs were the same. Even the paintings on the wall were the same. One difference was the telegraph machine sitting on the corner of the desk. The other was the large file cabinet bursting with papers.

Mr. Brighton walked over to the file cabinet and put his hand on the top drawer. He turned to Kevork and said, "What is the family name of your betrothed?"

"Hovsepian," Kevork replied.

"A very common name," said Mr. Brighton. He bent down and pulled out the second drawer, then began to flip through the papers filed under *H*. "What is her first name?"

"Marta."

Mr. Brighton's head jerked up. "Did you say Marta Hovsepian?"

"Yes," said Kevork. His heart was pounding in his chest. Why was the name so familiar to this man? Was that a good thing or bad?

"And had she lived at this orphanage before the deportations?"

"Yes," said Kevork. "And she had a younger brother, Onnig, and an older sister, Mariam."

Mr. Brighton's face exploded into a grin. "She is here!" he said.

"She is alive and well and healthy!" Then he ran over to Kevork and grabbed him by the arm. "Come. Let me take you to her now!"

Kevork was stunned. All this time. All of these years of wondering and hoping...

"Wh-when did she arrive?" he asked.

"Two years ago," answered Mr. Brighton. "She was one of the first adult survivors to come to the orphanage."

She had come back to the orphanage just as she said she would. Yet Kevork had never known. Did none of his telegrams get through?

Or perhaps there was another reason. Perhaps she didn't want him to know? He twisted the wedding ring on his little finger.

"Has she married?" he asked.

A strange look passed over Mr. Brighton's face. "Ah. No. She is not married."

Kevork sat down heavily on the chair in front of Mr. Brighton's desk, his head in his hands.

"This is so much to get used to," he said finally.

Mr. Brighton perched at the edge of his desk. He opened his mouth as if to say something more, but then he stopped. Finally, Kevork looked up at him, "Please," he said. "Take me to her."

Twenty-seven

MARTA

Marta sat wearily at the battered wooden desk in front of the classroom. Rows of children sat quietly, their heads down in concentration as they attempted to answer questions on the arithmetic quiz she had just handed out. The children in her class were the lucky ones. They were all now disease-free, well fed, and eager to learn. Although some were as young as four and others were older, they were all learning basic addition and subtraction. There was so much for them to learn. And there were now enough adults at the orphanage who spoke Armenian and Turkish well enough to teach them.

As the children wrote down their answers with admirable concentration, Marta did a head count. Fifty-nine. Everyone was here today. A good sign.

She opened the ledger book on her desk and put a check mark beside each student's name. Many of these children had arrived barely a month before, speaking only Turkish. In some cases, they spoke no real language at all, but a conglomeration of words and phrases from several languages. Yet it amazed her how quickly they learned once they were cleaned and fed.

But it was exhausting work. She taught them each morning, six days a week. Then the children went off to join their various squadrons, sorting clothing, making shoes, helping with the laundry, and helping in the kitchen. If it weren't for the labor of these healthy orphans, all of the others would never get the care and treatment they required.

Once class ended, Marta would go on to other duties too. Both she and Mariam did the bulk of the translating at the orphanage, and Marta supervised the daily laundry routine. And with thousands of children, the laundry was a monumental task.

Just then, Marta heard a light tap on her door. She looked up as it opened. Mr. Brighton stepped in. He had a silly grin on his face. She held her finger up to her lips and pointed to the children. She didn't want them to be disturbed. He gestured for her to join him. His behavior seemed odd, she thought. But after a look to make sure the children were occupied with their quiz, she went to meet him.

He grabbed her hand and pulled her outside, then he stepped into the classroom, closing the door silently behind him. She was about to go back in to see what this was all about. But then she saw the man outside the door.

Her heart skipped a beat.

"Kevork?"

She blinked, thinking maybe the mirage would disappear. But there he stood—taller and with a leathered brown face and unusual blue tattooed dots on either side of his forehead. It was undeniably her Kevork.

Her knees gave way and she almost stumbled to the ground, but he caught her. She wrapped her arms around one of his and clung to it, feeling sinewy muscles beneath the weathered cloth.

"You…you have come back," she said.

"Is there somewhere we can talk in privacy?"

Marta's mind was filled with a jumble of thoughts and emotions. A place to talk…a place of privacy? That was hard to come by. "Mr. Brighton's office," she said.

As they walked together through the orphanage complex, Marta clung to Kevork's arm for support. She never wanted to let him go again. She never wanted him out of her sight. She was oblivious to the people who walked past them—a cluster of chattering orphans, Dr. Thomas, who regarded her with a strange expression, and a white veiled nurse carrying a bundle of fresh bedding.

When they got to Mr. Brighton's office, Kevork closed the door behind them. He turned the guest chair sideways and gently lowered her into it. Then he pulled Mr. Brighton's chair from behind the desk and set it in front of her. He sat down and leaned toward her, their knees touching.

She wanted to wrap her arms around him, afraid that he might disappear again. But instead her hands fell to her lap. His hands. There was a wedding ring on his little finger. Had he married?

She watched, stunned, as he pulled the wedding ring off his little finger and placed it in his palm. He held the ring out to her.

"Will you marry me?" he asked.

She had hoped for it, prayed for it, for so long. Marta felt the comforting warmth of his knees through the fabric of her skirt. She looked into his eyes and then back to the simple brass wedding ring resting in his hand. It was the same kind of ring that her own father had given her mother. The same kind of wedding ring that her mother had died wearing. Her dear mother, Parantzim.

Pauline.

She looked into Kevork's eyes as her own filled with tears. She couldn't accept his offer of marriage now. He didn't know the truth.

She reached over, and with her two small hands she folded his fingers over the small brass wedding ring. His hand was now a fist. She breathed in deeply and blinked the tears out of her eyes.

"I want to marry you," she said. "But I don't know if you will still have me."

"Is there someone else?" Kevork asked, his voice trembling with emotion.

"There was someone else," said Marta. "But you are the only man I have ever loved. I...I have a daughter. Will you come with me to see her?"

At first he didn't understand. He searched her eyes to find the truth, but what he saw was unfathomable pain. What had she suffered through while he was gone? He had been in the concentration camps. He had seen firsthand what many women had survived.

Marta stood up.

He got to his feet and took her hand in his. She started for the door, but he pulled her into his arms and hugged her gently, her head resting on his chest.

"First, I want to know if you will marry me," he said. Then he held her as he felt her body shake with tears.

"But you haven't even asked me how this happened," she said.

"You will tell me when you are ready," he replied. "The important thing is that you survived."

Then he lifted her chin and asked her again.

"Yes," she said.

He hadn't judged. He had simply accepted it. After all these years of sadness and resignation, she could hardly believe that it was true.

"Come," he said. "Take me to see our daughter."

210